MW01595735

S. M. BAILEY

STRAIGHT AHEAD, IN THE DARK

A NOVEL

1

CreateSpace Independent Publishing Platform
First trade paperback edition November 2015

ISBN 978-1517730079

For Sarah, Shane, and Lucy

In memory of Stephen Emil Oslund (1970-2010), whom I have never met, but had given me so much.

STRAIGHT AHEAD, IN THE DARK

PART I
LAMENTING THE GHOST

The air is warm. It is a comfortable, bright day in late July, despite the calm winds. I am securing the last of my possessions in the bed of my green Dodge Dakota Sport. This truck is the last reminder of my grandfather, who passed away seven years earlier. He'd given me a few thousand dollars toward the sticker, so it carries hefty value to me as I carefully tie a strap over my life that is neatly fit into six or seven U-Haul boxes. Well, I'm lying. I left some stuff in a 5 x 10 storage locker so I can pick them up later. For the sake of this trip, I'm just taking my essentials: clothes, books, a few Pink Floyd CD's, and my notebooks that contain my drawings, songs and writings that have gotten me through "The Twenty-Seven Year Storm," as I like to call it.

Dad appears from the side of the house. This is a man that has been through a divorce and the death of not one, but TWO wives. One of which was my mother, whom by the accounts of many drunken nights, is the love of his life. I never knew what that felt like until about three months ago. But I'll get to that.

He stands in the sun, and watches me finish tighten the load. He will turn seventy in December. Seeing him there in the sun, I see him as an old man for the first time. He wears navy cotton shorts, and an AFC Champion Buffalo Bills t-shirt from 1993. I only know Dad as a bald man. He lost most of his hair in his early thirties. I can see this is hurting him despite the constant approval he has given me for this decision I have made. I can't count the times he told me to move away if I get the opportunity. *If you ever get the chance to get out of Niagara Falls, do it. There's nothing here for you anymore. Nothing left for anyone.* Throughout my life, he taught me to be strong. *You gotta pull up your socks, Roscoe. Only Shorty can take care of Shorty.* Sometimes, I'm too strong to the point that I have become a bit cold in my demeanor over the years.

"I'm just about done, ol' man." I say, tending to the straps.

"You got everything you're gonna take this trip? What's left in the garage?"

"I took everything of mine in the garage. Your garage is now Shorty-free."

This makes him laugh. For all the shit he has been through in his life, he still laughs. This makes me feel good. Shorty is my family nickname, despite being the tallest Benton male of 5'11", accompanied with a 185 pound frame of lean beef.

"Now I hope your brother and sister can pick up their shit so I can have my garage back." He doesn't mean that. He likes storing his kids' random garbage. It means we have to come back and visit him. He talks a mean game about us kids always being around. I've heard him say a hundred times; *I'm tired of storing everybody's underwear.* But I know him by now to say deep down he loves it. It makes him feel needed.

"I can't help you there." I answer. I finish my ties and walk around the truck to say goodbye. The sun is cooking the side of my head.

"So how long of a drive ya got?" Dad asks.
"Ten hours."

"And where ya movin to again?" He is making small talk. I had told him fifteen times this past week.

"Mebane, it's about thirty miles west of Durham."

"Oh yeah, that's right." He sweeps a hand over his shiny head.

"It's not like I'm leaving forever. I'll be back to visit. All the time, I promise."

"I know. I know."

He wouldn't look me in the eye. His demeanor makes me feel like a criminal. I feel horrible, like I'm abandoning him. "Well, I'll call you when I get there. And I will call you every weekend. It'll be great! I just have to do this."

"Ok." His gaze is at the sidewalk while he slowly shuffles his naked feet.

I open the driver door and look back in his direction. He stands in the sun with a pained look on his face still making an effort to avoid eye contact.

"I'll see you later." I said. "I love you." I can't remember the last time I told him I loved him.

He takes a few steps backward, and raises his hand to wave goodbye. "I love you too." With his head down, still waving, he disappears behind the house.

I stand in the driveway with the Dodge, alone in the July sun, and my eyes start to water. *What the hell is wrong with me?!?* I think. *I'm finally doing something good with my life and I feel like shit.*

I climb in the truck and slam the door. I take one final look at the back yard of the house I grew up in. Somehow I know I will never live here again. My Dad will until he dies because he is a creature of preservation. He owns it outright. This is the house he bought with my mother in 1978, the year of my birth. It is an old dwelling built in the 1860's, converted from an old barn. The house next door used to be the farmhouse that the barn belonged to. I start the truck, give a final salute to the empty back yard, and head down the driveway.

It doesn't take long for me to feel uncomfortable. Sixty-Fifth Street is no longer my home. *It's my old stomping grounds.* I drive past the HUGE poplar tree on the corner of Edison Avenue where Ricky Lomax and Danny Caldecott, taking turns swinging a Louisville slugger like an ax, smashed a hole in the bark the size of a basketball. The scar left on the tree had shrunk over the years to the size of a handprint. Christ, I have a story about that day. But I'll get to that later.

Further down the road, stands Mr. Mundo's house, where I kissed Kim Carey on the cheek behind his garage. It's funny what goes through your brain when you are leaving your hometown to start a new life. I haven't thought of that in years. I drive past the part in the street where the neighborhood kids used to play football. You needed two completions for a first down, and the field consisted of a length of street between two electrical poles. Looking at it now, it looks about twenty-five yards long. When you're eight, it looked long enough for a full football field. The field at the end of the block is where I threw as many touchdown passes in about three years as Brett Favre did his entire NFL career. I had a rocket arm. I let that dream fade away. I don't regret it though. But I'll tell you one thing, I will go to my grave believing whole heartedly that I'm a better quarterback than Tom Brady. And there are a few people I know that can back that up. Sixty-Fifth Street is a block from Interstate 90, which is the route I am using to leave Niagara Falls behind, somewhere between good luck and goodbye.

2

The Grand Island Bridge crosses the Niagara River, which of course, feeds the Bridal Veil, American, and Horseshoe portions of Niagara Falls. The weather is beautiful, even on a sticky July day, when I look to my right and see the mist rising from the waterfalls in the distance. I have taken that for granted for sure. I haven't visited the waterfalls in a few years and I live here. Well, not anymore. This bridge has seen some action over the years I can tell ya. I spent many of blazing hot summer days with my best friend, Mack Bones, jumping off this bridge into the Niagara River. The first time you jump, your stomach feels like it hits the back of your throat because you're so high up. There is a catwalk that runs the length of the bridge and it is anywhere from twenty to eighty feet to the water. Mack and I were bad asses so we would go about one third of the way in and jump from the catwalk about forty feet up. The river is on average ten feet deep. Under the bridge it is about nine, so you immediately hit the bottom and push to the surface. In late summer, the seaweed is thick and slimy. It's quite a strange feeling swimming through nine feet of thick, warm, wet seaweed. This far into summer, I can see the water turning a deep green down there.

I once knew this girl in my gym class in high school. One day I ran into her walking down Buffalo Avenue and spent a few hours shooting the shit. We ended up climbing onto the catwalk, and *doing the business.* Cars and trucks drove over our head, having no idea what was going on underneath them as they drove down the interstate.

To the left of the bridge is a little creek mouth that empties into the river. The waterway that's attached is Woods Creek. My brother and I spent many Saturday mornings catching fish there with Dad. Over the years, when Junior got older and had other things to do, that left my dad and me on those Saturday mornings for a few years. I cherish those moments with him. I don't remember all of them but they are real special to me. We did that until I was probably eleven or twelve. I wish we had never stopped. When Dad and I were alone fishing together, I felt safe, like nothing would ever hurt us.

Just over the bridge, I pay the toll—a fucking dollar, damn New York State—and head out on the interstate toward my new life. The sun is now hot as hades so I roll down the windows. The air conditioning had given out some time over the winter and when I fired it up the first time this summer, the air coming out of the vents was as cold as the Death Valley wind at high noon. So I have to deal with the wind factor blasting through my truck driving sixty to seventy miles per hour. But I don't mind. It's better than baking in my seat with the windows up sweating balls. I can't wait to get to the other side of this road trip. There's something exciting about up and leaving your home town. Sure, I'm leaving my family and friends behind. That will hurt the most. Friends fade away over the years, especially when you move out of state. First you come back after a few months to visit. Then it's a year later. After a while, you're reduced to a quick e-mail hello or a like on your Facebook status. I'm going to miss my boys I hung out with the past half dozen years and will cherish the crazy times we had. A bunch of characters they are. Like the USA Network, *characters welcome*.

As long as I live, if I have my way, I have just left Niagara Falls as a citizen for the last time.

3

The last memory of my mother was when she was in the hospital a week before she died. At the time, I had no idea why she was there. I just remember going with my dad—don't ask me what we drove in—to Niagara Falls Memorial Medical Center to visit her. I remember she was in bed; a tube was sticking in her hand and snaking down the sheets.

"What's that?" I asked, pointing to the contraption. It was foreign to me. I looked at it like it was an alien tentacle.

"Oh, it's just medicine." She replied. "It's to make me feel all better." It was a sweet generic answer to satisfy her naïve son.

A few days earlier, my dad had found my mother on her knees, leaning against the dining room table. He was getting ready for work that particular evening when he strolls out of the bedroom door and into a scene of panic. This was the exact moment the weather changed for me. He knew something wasn't right so he walked her outside to the front porch to get some fresh air. She didn't sound right, and she was having a hard time talking. After about twenty minutes, he didn't feel convinced that all was normal so he drove her to the hospital.

I stared at the tube taped to her hand. The doctor was talking to Dad in the corner and I couldn't hear what they were saying. They mumbled away about medical terms. My mother was paying attention to them as I kept staring at that alien tentacle. There was a clear solution in it. I remember thinking that this was all boring and I wanted to be home watching cartoons. How could I have known this would be my last memory of her? If I had known this, I would have wanted to be there. I still want to be there.

Dad met Sandrea Beck at a restaurant she was waitressing at in 1976. He was thirty-five, and was going through a bitter divorce and custody battle for his three kids. She was twenty-eight, and had moved back home to Niagara Falls to start a new life after a rough relationship during her college days at RIT in Rochester. She had thick wavy red hair like Shirley MacLaine. As a matter of fact, she resembled her. My mother was 5'8", tall for a woman, and what you would consider an amazon. She was just as beautiful as she was strong and brave. My dad was smitten with her, but she was reluctant to start a relationship with a guy with all this baggage. But Dad was a smooth operator, a real charmer with the ladies. When he had an interest in a woman, he was confident and cool, and the ladies ate it up. My mother was no different, baggage or not.

They started dating during the summer of '76 and things progressed. The biological clock was ticking in my mother—more like ROARING—and my dad was NOT thrilled about having a fourth child. Well, my mother was also a persuasive one, and got what she wanted when she needed to. She wanted a child before she turned thirty. They married on Valentine's Day. A little more than three months later, I was born on Wednesday, May 31, 1978. My mother turned thirty in July.

Dad had two daughters and a son from his previous marriage and from day one, I was their brother; none of this half-brother, red-headed step-child business. I am their brother, period. Despite that, to this day, I always felt like I was an outsider. I can't explain it. I always felt I was in the way. They had inside jokes I was never a part of. It wasn't anything they did or anything that they meant to do. They included me in everything. All their most intimate moments in life, I was a part of and I will always be grateful. But, I felt different.

I have few memories of my mother. I remember one time I awoke from a bad dream so I went and climbed into my parents' bed with them. I remember it was warm and cozy. My mother was sleeping and her head was craned in a weird position so I could fit between her and Dad. She was considerate like that. I heard various stories of how I was her world, and how much she loved me. She would pain herself so I could be taken care of.

People talked of how great of a person she was. She loved my sisters and brother even though they weren't her children biologically. They'd say she was an angel and things like, *Gee Shorty, it's such a shame you don't remember her.* I would get so mad and wonder why it was me that deserved to not have my mother. Why I deserved to not remember how a mother's love for their son felt. I would curse God. *Damn him. Fuck this guy. How dare he take my mother?* This is one of the reasons I've come to the conclusion that he doesn't exist. But I'm not going to get into that. That is a whole other can of worms.

So, the doctor released her. The doctor determined she had a blood clot in her brain but it wasn't too serious. They would keep an eye on it every few months, and if it's still there in a year, they would operate.

A week later, on Thursday, I was at Pre-K. It was a nice spring day. I remember this like it was last week. There are certain things that are blurry but for the most part, this day will live with me forever.

I was standing on the sidewalk like a statue in the cool spring air at Riverside Presbyterian Church on Eighty-Fifth Street. My mother's routine consisted of dropping me off in the morning around eight o'clock, visiting my Aunt Lou and Uncle Lee on South Avenue downtown for a few hours or run errands, then picking me back up at noon. She was on medical leave from her job as a secretary at Carborundum, a company that refined silicon carbide. Cars one by one pulled up to the sidewalk and little by little the other Pre-K kids left. I couldn't tell you how long I stood there, my feet fixed to the concrete. After a while, a car full of ladies pulled over in front of me. My Pre-K teacher—I can't recall her name—leaned over her passenger and flashed her smile at me. She was such a sweet lady; a mandatory prerequisite for her line of work.

"Do you need a ride Stephen?" She asked.

"No, Mommy picks me up." By then I was fidgeting in place.

"Is she running late sweetie?"

"I dunno."

"Well, we will just wait here until she arrives so you're safe, ok?"

I looked down the deserted road watching for anything familiar, like Mom's car. "Ok."

And they did. I remember waiting there for a little while longer. I assume they knew it was getting late so they offered me a ride home. She was my teacher, and she was a person that I trusted so I didn't think twice about getting a ride from her. I remember sitting between the two ladies in the back seat, and it was quiet. Almost like they knew something was not right. Of course I was oblivious to anything that was going on; being a month before my fifth birthday. We are all oblivious at that age. I cannot tell you why I remember so much about that day. Maybe I was afraid, and fear seems to stick with you at times. I remember getting home and my brother, Junior, was already there. He was two months shy of his tenth birthday. He was a lanky kid with knobby knees, and hair so blond his head looked like a Q-Tip. School let out at three, so the timeline had put us at about three-thirty, four o'clock. I stood out in front of that church and waited a good few hours for my mother who never showed.

There were two children under the age of ten at home, alone. I told Junior my mother did not pick me up and I got a ride home from my teacher. I remember as I talked he kept looking out the front door windows in hopes that my mother would show up. It was one of those thick brown wooden jobs, with three small windows in a stepped down pattern. He was only tall enough to look out of the last one. After I finished telling my tale of desertion, he called Dad at work.

"Hi Dad, something's wrong, Sandy didn't come home." Junior said to the phone. My siblings called my mom Sandy. I once did also and she got so mad at me. It's understandable. She wanted a child so bad and once I showed up, I didn't call her Mom, I called her Sandy.

There was a pause.

"She's not here."

Pause.

"I don't know. He said his teacher dropped him off."

Pause.

"Ok, bye." He hung up the phone. It was one of the old black rotary ones with the clear circular dial on the front.

"He says he's coming home."

That was the last thing I remember of Thursday, April 21, 1983.

4

The phone rang. My dad and his best friend Denny Bones was in the kitchen. Denny, a police officer for the City of Buffalo was a dear family friend who had known my father since they were in grade school. They pulled an all-nighter searching the city for my mother. Dad called to report my mother missing but authorities couldn't help yet because it hadn't been twenty-four hours. Denny pulled some strings but they came up empty.

"Hello?" Dad answered.

"Hello Mr. Benton," the voice asked, "This is Dr. Rick Doss with the Niagara County coroners' office. I regret to inform you that your wife has expired."

Expired?!? Really? That's how it happens.

That's how you rip a grown man's heart out of his chest. There was no sympathy. There was no compassion. She was just another body found in a car, a block away from where she left Uncle Lee and Aunt Lou's house. It was just another call Dr. Doss had to make that day. Hell, he probably had to make a dozen calls just like that one.

Dad staggered, your legs tend to turn to rubber from hearing news like that. Denny steadied him. That's what best friends are for.

My mother had been visiting on South Avenue with my Aunt and Uncle the morning she went missing. The streets downtown are one-way, alternating East and West. She made a right on a cross street and then another right on Cleveland Avenue to head back in the direction toward Pre-K to pick me up. She never made it. A few houses down the blood clot in her head—the one the doctors said wasn't that serious—broke free causing an aneurysm. She tried to pull over, jumping the curb with the passenger side front wheel. The car came to rest in front of a house that was home to a registered nurse. The nurse looked out her bay window and seen a car illegally parked in front of her house. She had seen a woman in the driver's seat. She didn't think anything of it and went about her business. A little while later, she looked again and the car was empty. She actually left for work later in the evening, and the car was still there.

The story gets better. Apparently, through the night a cop had written a few parking tickets and stuck them under the windshield wiper. In the morning around nine o'clock, another cop stopped by the vehicle and noticed my mother lying across the front seats. She had been missing for twenty-two hours. According to the coroner, she had been dead for twelve. This means she was in the car alive for ten hours. She wasn't really. The aneurysm had rendered her brain dead.

I've seen my dad cry twice in my life. *Benton's don't cry, when you're as tough as we are!* This is probably why I don't cry often. Only a few people have seen me cry. After receiving the news, he made the rounds. Dad and I drove in the family Ford Escort to my oldest sister Petrisha's apartment down town. And being born in 1963, she was doomed with a name like Petrisha. I guess it's better than Moon Beam or something. The family calls her Pet. She was nineteen, with long straight dark hair, and as pretty as nineteen year olds are. She got pregnant by a guy named Marc and my nephew Jerald was born a month before my fourth birthday. Yes, I was a three-year-old uncle.

We arrived at Pet's apartment. It was the bottom level of a two family house. I followed Dad up the steps to her door where Pet was waiting for us. Toddler toys and two lawn chairs cluttered the small porch that I remember had grey paint that flaked off the floor boards. Pet guided us inside and Dad told them the news. Dad walked away and disappeared through the kitchenette. Marc followed but punched a hole in the plaster by the door molding. I remember watching the pieces of plaster fall to the rug. I walked through the kitchenette and made a left toward the bedrooms. Straight ahead, in the dark, Dad sat on the toilet in the bathroom. He was sobbing softly; his right hand covering his eyes.

"What's wrong Daddy?" I asked, nudging his left arm. But he didn't answer me. He just sat there. I kept asking, "Daddy, Daddy, what's wrong?" He just sat there.

Marc walked in after a few minutes and took me away so Dad could be alone. You do not forget something like that. I don't recall that day afterward. I had a total of fifty-nine months with the greatest mother on the planet. But I wouldn't know. It's hardly enough time to really get to know and love your mother, especially at that age.

5

There is one thing I am very grateful for. Dad did not take me to see my mother at her funeral. Some years later he would tell me that he didn't want my last memory to be of her laid out in her coffin all dolled up. I would take the hospital memory over that any day of the week and twice on Sunday. Anything would have been better than that. I have thanked him many times. He had the raw deal. I cannot begin to imagine what he felt seeing the love of his life in a pine box.

I remember one event of that day. Dad was planning to take me for a ride.

"Hey Shorty, let's go for a ride." He requested.

"Where?"

"I wanna show ya somethin."

He knew I loved to go for a ride with him. When I was young, it was one of my favorite things to do. He had a tape of oldies music from the fifties called, "Blast from the Past," that he played in the cassette deck continuously. I used to love singing along to songs like, "It's all in the Game" by Tommy Edwards, and "The Great Pretender" by The Platters.

We walked out onto the back porch where the concrete edges were rounded and crumbled away with age. He stopped in the muddy patch at the foot of the steps. I looked at him befuddled.

"See those clouds there Shorty?" He asked, pointing at a cloud cluster in the sky.

"Yeah?"

"That's where Mommy has gone to live."

"Why?" I asked. "Didn't she like it here?"

"Yes, Shorty she did. But she had to go away. And when people have to go away, they live there." He pointed. "She's not coming back, ok?"

"Can we live there with her?"

"No. It doesn't work that way."

"I'm gonna miss her." I said, still mumbling through the English language.

"I know. I will too. Everyone will."

We never went for a ride that day. I remember I wasn't too upset about my mother going to live in the clouds either. How could I be upset? I was so naïve. I was thinking of the "Blast from the Past" tape. That's how simply you tell a boy who was almost five that his mother was never coming back. It was simple because I had no idea what *she's not coming back* had meant. It was simple because I was still simple, and everything was simple when you're five.

A few months later I got the same story. But it was my grandmother that went to live in the place in the clouds. She was of German descent but you wouldn't know it by looking at her. My mother was the mirror image of her, and of course she reminded me of Mom. I was devastated. The fear crept in from everywhere. People I love were going away. I started to fear my dad and my brother and sisters were next. I didn't want them to leave, even to go to the store without me. It was a very difficult time for everyone. I was confused as to why this was happening. The cloud story was the best way Dad could help me understand. How do you tell a five year old boy that you do not live forever? How do you tell him we're only here for a small window in time? The conundrum Dad must have had to face.

6

My Uncle had three daughters. One got married in July, and I was asked to be the ring bearer at the wedding. I had no idea what a ring bearer was. I was just excited to hang out with my cousins. Like my sisters and brother, they were older than I, and they loved their little cute cousin. For months, there were plans and rehearsals and cake tastings and wedding dress fittings. My mother's death had thrown a wrench in the soup.

When the day came, it was supposed to be a great day of celebration, with warm times and love in the air. The church was this huge monstrosity of a building, decorated like something out of a movie. I was wearing a black tuxedo with a red tie and cummerbund. Barely five, fate had wound back with its steel-toed boots and kicked me square in the teeth. My mother—Aunt Sandy—was no longer here and it was felt throughout the day. When it came time for me to walk out during the wedding march, instead of going straight down the aisle like everyone else, I caught a glimpse of Dad at the end of a pew half way down so I drifted toward him. Marching and drifting. Marching and drifting. When I arrived at his pew, he set me straight and directed me toward the front of the church. So with all this emotion, how I looked and drifting toward Dad, I brought the whole church to its knees. There wasn't a dry eye in the place. That day was all too much. I vaguely remember drifting down the aisle. After the wedding, at the reception, I got a plush Mickey Mouse that was bigger that I was for my wedding party present. I do remember this. I was thrilled. I had it for years.

7

Dad enrolled me in kindergarten that fall. I have a picture of me on the first day holding my Tom and Jerry book bag in the front yard. I loved that book bag. I love that picture actually. That September wasn't good to my dad. He was laid off at his job at Arco Sphere, where he had been a shift supervisor. They did something with metals, I don't recall.

My dad, newly unemployed and trying to raise four kids on his own, would get me up in the morning and make me breakfast. We would watch Green Acres reruns, while he packed my lunch in a brown paper bag. He would stand at the bus stop, drinking his morning coffee, while we waited for the school bus together. That was our routine for a while.

From a young age, I loved art. *You were born with that drawing talent shit, Shorty.* Dad would say. *It's just in you.* There is an art museum called, The Castellani Art Museum, in Niagara Falls, and throughout my life I've had a few drawings shown there. They're big on local talent. So when a school kid has a stroke of genius and draws something just short of awesome, their art teachers would send the kids work to the art museum and show it for a weekend. It's kind of cool in my opinion.

Drawing was a way for me to cope with my mother being gone. I would disappear into my drawings for a while. It was a way to escape reality. But that didn't last long. The pain infiltrated first grade art class, where I wore one of Dad's old t-shirts that hung to my shins, for a smock. It smelled like him for a while and I could still remember it.

"Today, we are drawing a member of your family!" The teacher said. I remember she was a tall fit lady, probably around my mother's age, thirty-five. "I'll show you how, just copy what I do. Ok guys?"

Man, I loved art class. It was something I was good at, and people were happy about what I drew. I wasn't Picasso of course, but I was better than the average six year old.

"First, you draw a big uppercase U. You know how to do that right? You know how to draw an upper case U?" She asked us. She made her rounds helping us kids as she went. But not me, I was a natural!

"Ok, you ready for the next step? Let's draw a face, eyes, nose, and mouth. If you are drawing your mother or sister, give her red lipstick on her lips! See how nice that is?" She drew her example as she taught. I copied hers to a T. I gave mine nice ears that were proportional. She even showed us to draw a plus in the big upper case U and use that to let us know where to draw the facial features. Mine was right on. Danny Caldecott was next to me. I remember mine was better than his, and we were laughing because the face he was drawing looked funny; *like a Picasso.*

"Next, let's draw some hair!" She exclaimed excitedly. I think she was more excited than we were! I drew the face of my mom of course. So I drew red curly hair in big swoopy strokes. It ended up looking like Shirley Temple rather that Shirley MacLaine, but who's paying attention right?

When I was finished I was proud of it. It was symmetrical and it resembled a human face. Maybe not my mothers' face, but it was a face with red hair and brown eyes. In my eyes it was a picture of my mother. I remember thinking how much I wanted her to see it. The teacher was coming around and commenting on all the drawings. She came to Danny's and said, "Wow, that's interesting Daniel. Who is this supposed to be?"

"I Dunno. I was drawin stuff." We giggled at it. She made her way to my portrait. She was immediately impressed.

"Oh my good lord Stephen!" She was a religious lady. "Who is this supposed to be?"

"My mom." I said.

"This is beautiful Stephen. When your mother sees this, she is gonna FLIP OUT!" She made this grand sweeping circular gesture with her right hand. I froze. I wanted to whisper to her that my mother will not see this portrait because she died. But I couldn't do it. I didn't want the sympathy. I didn't want her to look down on me with sorrow and express how sorry she was to hear that. I didn't want her to say she merely didn't know my circumstances. I didn't want any of it. I just wanted this pain to stop. Before I got on the bus to go home that afternoon, I ripped up the picture and threw it away. I couldn't look at it.

That was the moment in my life where I made a conscious decision to just forget about everything. *I don't remember*. No, I don't remember going shopping with my mother. I don't remember my mother doing that. I don't remember going there with my mother. *I don't remember.*

Sadly, it worked. To this day I have very little recollection of my mother. I wish I hadn't done that. But I was six. I guess that is how a six year old copes with his mothers' death.

8

Dad started dating a nice Italian lady named Cora Pontini in late 1983. She was the deli clerk at the 7-Eleven a few blocks away from our house. Dad stopped there every morning for a coffee and the morning paper. When my mother passed away, Cora knew Dad as the regular who had just lost his wife to a sudden brain aneurysm as she would come to find out through the neighborhood gossipers. I have little recollection of this period in time. I just remember going with Dad every Friday afternoon to the unemployment office to pick up his check.

Cora seemed really nice. She was thick and curvy, with olive skin that tanned like a perfect kiss from the sun. Her hair was dark and curly, just past her shoulders, and never a strand out of place. She was the same age as my mother and knew of her. I believe it was Freud who said men search for their mother in the perfect woman. Cora is the reason I have such a love for Italian women. Italian women have an exotic sway to them. They cook better.

They tan like a dream, and their as gorgeous as white sand on a tropical beach.

The Benton family had had a shitty year, and so had Cora. She'd just gone through the wringer from a messy divorce. She caught her husband banging her best friend. That's a two for one slam in the face from where I come from. So anyway, Dad the widower and Cora the divorcée hit it off. Dad being the seasoned drinker that he was would take Cora to his favorite gin mills around Niagara Falls and Donald Junction. She wasn't a drinker. She would try to be a trooper and keep up with him to no avail. Cora learned the pain of a hang-over the hard way.

Dad told Cora to go and make Christmas of 1983 the best damn Christmas anyone had ever seen. I bet it was to help everyone forget about the year for a few short hours. That morning, Junior and I, and our sister Sonya awoke to a mountain of gifts the size of the Himalayas. The whole front wall of the living room was covered in gifts wrapped in red and green paper. We received footballs, baseballs with gloves and bats, G.I. Joes, Rubik's Cubes, and games like Risk, Clue, and Life from Santa Claus that year. Sonya got cassette tapes of her favorite bands, Stephen King books, and designer clothes galore. We got candy and chocolate. Junior and I received remote control cars. We even got model cars to assemble and glue together.

For the briefest of moments we did forget about the year, and it was good. It was good for a while.

1984 was a decent year. Dad scored a job at the Waste Water Treatment Plant downtown and the stability came back to our little family unit. That summer Dad had a surprise for us.

Junior and I were watching Transformers one Saturday morning. Optimus Prime was our best friend and we lived his adventures right by his side.

"So you guys like Cora?" Dad breezed in the living room and sat next to us on the couch. He had a steaming mug in his hand which smelled of Arabica beans.

"Yeah, she's cool." Junior answered.

"Yeah, she's cool." I repeated. Junior shot me a look and punched me in the arm.

"I want to ask her to marry me. Do you think I should?" We both shot off the couch and ran to the back door to put our shoes on. "Easy, EASY!" Dad shouted in our direction. We ran out the back door and through the front yard. "Where are you going?!?"

We ran three blocks to 7-Eleven in our pajamas. We were winded like two marathon runners by the time we arrived and asked Cora for Dad. We were so happy. She was surprised to say the least but she accepted. It was a good time. They were married in November by a Justice of the Peace. Junior and I were the only witnesses. Things were close to normal again. I didn't have my mother, but I liked Cora a whole lot so this marriage was fine by me.

9

My mother's father used to come over every Sunday to have coffee with my dad. He was a wiry man of German descent with hands the size of frying pans. His wardrobe consisted of green Dickie's mechanics pants, plain white shirts, and his suit he wore for his masonic meetings. He had the same buzz cut since the day he enlisted. In World

War II he was a mechanic for Patton and his "Hell on Wheels" Tank Brigade. He was a man's man that loved baseball and hunting, and he was never without a pocket knife. Before I was born, a stroke left half of his tongue paralyzed so he had a hard time speaking.

We kept special coffee just for him. I would sit at the breakfast bar eating my corn flakes and listen to them talk about adult stuff like city politics and taxes. Grandpa used to own a garage that specialized in transmission repair, which was now operated by my uncle since his retirement. I loved it. What boy doesn't like hanging out with his Dad and Grandpa? It was the highlight of my week.

Some Sundays, after his visit, I would go with Grandpa and have breakfast with him. He was a 33rd degree Mason, Scottish Rite, Knights Templar, you name it. He even had a Templar sword. He would take me to the blue lodge he belonged to where they would put on pancake breakfasts every third Sunday. That was a blast. After a while, because I would ask for seconds, they made special pancakes for me. My breakfast consisted of a stack of three pancakes, which were the size of dinner plates, and a second plate full of eggs and sausage. These old guys loved me and would sit at our table, talk of old times and comment about how I could put it away. Grandpa would sit at the table feeling proud of me. *He will make a fine brother someday.*

The truth was Cora for some reason thought I didn't need much food and I was making up for it at these breakfasts. On the weekends, maybe out of laziness, who knows, I would normally have a bowl of cereal in the morning. But she refused to make me lunch, so I was constantly asking for lunch at my buddies house, which got old real quick. At dinner, I rarely got seconds when I asked for them. Maybe we weren't as well off as I thought, I don't know. But Cora constantly went to bingo over the border in Canada, and more than a handful of times got lucky enough to win the jackpot which was usually between one and three thousand dollars. I was painfully skinny and a growing boy. She would constantly cut smaller pieces for me whenever we ordered out pizza. I never understood this. I grew to know hunger pains.

Cora was a fantastic cook. Her parents were from Italy and moved to the States back in the early forties, so she learned from the best. She made everything from scratch and her spaghetti sauce was legendary. I loved her cooking. If I sit still and really think about it, I can still taste her stuffed shells. Even then with all this great food around, she would ration it to me like I was a refugee.

10

While the Iran-Contra affair was breaking open all over the place, my two sisters by that time lived on their own, and came home to visit often. I would come down stairs and say hi, just to be sent back upstairs by Cora like some disease or something she was ashamed of. My sisters never dared to say anything in fear of not being able to comeback. Dad never spoke up either. I was not allowed to hang out down stairs for any reason. I couldn't understand why she was doing this all of a sudden. I was allotted a half hour before bed to watch television. Whatever was on that Dad wanted to watch, that was my option. I used to be able to watch as much as I wanted. It was like I was being grounded. But for what, who knew.

I wouldn't dare to say a word, because if it was something that aggravated her for any reason—which was a lot apparently—she would reach over and smash me in the mouth. She bloodied my lip many times for *giving her lip* she called it. It was one of her favorite things to do. That and pull my hair until my scalp hurt. I felt neglected and no one stood up for me. She suddenly had free reign over me and I was confused to what I had done to deserve it. I just couldn't make her happy; ever.

That summer I elected to shave my head when I needed a haircut. Cora joked that she couldn't grab my hair anymore. That was the point, little did she know. But she promptly told me that she could find a way if I stepped out of line. She liked to squeeze my arm while digging her long nails into my skin. I grew to hate those nails and later, the person attached to them.

After school I could go out and play until dinner. If my buddies were busy, I would play football by myself by catching self-thrown rainbow passes and handing off to imaginary running backs, or throwing passes to trees. If the ball hit the tree, the pass was complete and the receiver was immediately tackled right at that spot. I did play-by-play color commentary for these single man games. I made rules and first down markers. People around the neighborhood thought I was probably a little off. I did this so I wouldn't have to stay upstairs. It was making me crazy. Reading and drawing, my favorite pastimes, only took up so much time. I was constantly getting grounded for the littlest mundane things so it was weighing on me. Junior was very active in sports in high school and he was always off at a practice, or with friends. So I was left alone up there a lot.

Dad would have a few beers after work with his co-workers two, three, sometimes four nights a week. He would come home drunk or buzzed, and after a brief argument with Cora, go fall asleep on the couch until dinner. She would wake him, he would eat, then go right back to the couch after dinner. Later he would watch television, with Cora, Junior, and me, *for the half hour I was allotted*, and then go to bed. That was his routine for years. The only time I could hang out with him was on the weekends in the garage. He would putter around having a few beers, *totties* he called them, while I watched. These are the times we would talk about school and he would teach me life lessons. I would have loved to ask him why he let Cora abuse me like she did. But I never had the courage. He would have sided with her anyway. *You always have a boss in life, at work, or at school*, he would say. *There are rules to follow. You will find out as you grow up. Your time will come.* And FUCK, he always said that. *Your time will come.* Why did Dad let Cora discipline me? She wasn't my mother. She never had kids of her own so she had no idea.

Seth, an annoying kid that lived next door, was a jerk to me all the time. He was one of those kids that hung out with the bullies and trouble makers, but wasn't one of them; a wannabe. One time he set up a fort in the adjacent field by our houses with old rugs and a reclining chair. So, Ricky Lomax and I trashed it. There was a box of crayons in the fort so with one of those crayons, on the overturned recliner in thick red letters I wrote, SETH IS AN ASSHOLE!!!!!

The next afternoon Cora met me in the front yard after school with a spray bottle filled with water and a sponge. Seth had written ASSHOLE SETH BY BENTON with green crayon on a panel under his porch that conveniently faced our house. As an added touch he threw the crayon just over our fence a few feet away from their porch. I don't think Cora was that stupid to buy this whole set up. But since she was in the position to do so, to teach me a lesson in manners, who knows, she made me scrub it off. Even after I pleaded my case that there was no way I would have wrote it in a place Dad and Cora could see it, let alone write my last name on it—which I never used to call myself anyway—and fail to get rid of the crayon I used. She stood over me all smug as I scrubbed, and told me to *use elbow grease* with her cocky demeanor she dialed up every now and again to let me know who was boss.

11

Dad and I always made it to Junior's football games and swim meets at the high school. Junior grew up to be very athletic. He was chiseled like a Greek god and was great at what he did. Sometimes we would go to out of town schools to see him if they were close enough. I loved these times. Any time I could spend with my dad and brother without Cora around was fine by me. Dad didn't miss Junior's sporting events for anything. Whatever he was into, Dad was there. But Dad didn't go to any of my school functions. I was in chorus and I acted in school plays a lot. Cora made those functions. She was so sweet in public. She was a completely different person. She would talk me up like I was the next Robert Redford or Neil Diamond. But once we got back home, I had a 50/50 shot of which Cora I was getting.

Dad rarely saw the abuse that I endured from Cora because he was on the couch most of the time. He didn't see the times she snapped and smashed me in the mouth with her wedding ring for the smallest details. She never wanted to see me. Except for the times Dad would be so drunk he would come home from work and go right to bed. Those were prime nights she would call up the stairs to me.

"Shorty."

I ran to the landing. There was a complete apartment upstairs. It was like Junior and I had our own bachelor pad. He used to stock the fridge with Gatorade and snacks that I constantly stole from him. The place was loaded with old style dark brown paneling. The balding rug was light brown and red like Rice-a-Roni Spanish rice. A measured cut of plywood and a sheet covered the top of the stove, where our television was set up.

"Yeah?"

"Wanna play Nintendo?" *Nen-tendo.*

"Sure!" I would exclaim, and all would be forgiven. Because I just wanted a mother, and while she was nice to me, she was perfect.

12

One day on the bus, I was being a shit on the ride home from school. It was not common knowledge to me, when a student was unruly on the bus, the driver or driver's aide sends what was called a "conduct referral" to your house. In the eighties, school buses had bus aides that roamed the bus and kept an eye out for the kids' safety and what not, while the driver made the rounds to the various stops. I don't know if they still do this but that was the common practice then.

A few weeks later, the day Danny and Ricky smashed a hole in the tree on the bus stop corner, Danny was recalling to Ricky what they had done that morning and I was sitting in the seat across the aisle listening in. We were dying of laughter listening to Danny tell the story of blasting away at the tree, *crankin homers out of the park*, to our friends on the bus. When the bus turned down Edison Avenue and our stop came into view, I looked down the aisle through the windshield and to my surprise found Cora standing at the corner.

"Is that Cora?" Ricky asked. I knew it was her.

"What is she doing there?" I asked him, knowing he had no idea.

"Who knows?" Questions were all around.

Over the years, they came to know Cora enough to know something was not right. The bus crept to a stop at the corner and the driver opened the doors. Danny, Ricky, and I, in that order filed out. Danny and Ricky proceeded across the front of that big yellow Twinkie and started down the street toward their houses.

"Hi." I said to her.

She didn't answer. Before I knew it, she grabbed me by my hair and started dragging me home three houses down from the corner. My feet barely touched the ground, like I was on a human hoist. Danny and Ricky witnessed the whole scene. By the time she dragged me in the house my scalp was already aching and sore. On the breakfast nook in the kitchen, she snatched a piece of paper and shoved it in my face.

"You see this?!?" She yelled. Her voice rattled in my eardrums. I'd come accostomed to her yelling. "This is a warning from the bus aide. This says you were disruptive on the bus last week, Monday, and repeatedly *defied* her when she requested you to settle down and sit in your seat. WHY WERE YOU ACTING THIS WAY?"

She used the word defied in the wrong context. If I would have said something, good god. I was already scared out of my mind. I knew she was going to beat me.

"I don't know!" I cried, wild eyed, waiting for her to strike, stuttered some inaudible jargon. She grabbed my mouth and dug her nails into my face.

"Don't say you don't know." She said through her teeth. "I can't stand when you say you don't know. You know damn well YOU KNOW!"

POW! She slapped me across the face and started slapping me over the head. I felt her heavy gold wedding ring cracking my head every time she slapped. It was so fast. I tried putting my hands up to shield the abuse but she just kept the barrage of smacks coming.

"Get your ass upstairs. LAME BRAIN!" She yelled. I ran upstairs to my bedroom crying with my burning cheek and aching scalp. My hate for her boiled over. Times like this I wished she would just drop dead. I wanted her to die. I wished her death. I welcomed it.

I thought that was the end of it, until Dad came home. Cora, like some informant, ratted me out. After a few minutes Dad trotted up the stairs. I sat on my bed reading when he came through the door. I was horrified. I knew what he came to do. He wound back and smacked me on the shoulder with his huge mitt. His hands looked like they were as big as a bunch of bananas anyway. I flew off my bed and slammed against the wall. He snatched me off the floor and bent me over his knee. He smacked my ass and it hurt so badly it took my breath away. I had both hands trying to block the pain that was coming. He finally peeled away my arms for a clean shot, pulled my pants down, and smacked me on my bare butt. I screamed bloody murder, and started bawling uncontrollably from the pain. He then threw me off his knee like a ragdoll.

"GET KICKED OFF THE BUS AND SEE WHAT HAPPENS TO YOU!" He yelled, and left my room storming down the stairs. Cora laid into him something awful. I heard them argue as I shook from my cries of anguish. Junior's head peaked out of his room and into mine.

"Why are you still crying? He left five minutes ago." I didn't answer. I could barely catch my breath.

"WHY DID YOU DO THAT?" I heard Cora yell. "I HAVE ALREADY TAKEN CARE OF IT. YOU SHOULD BEAT THAT OTHER LAME BRAINED SON OF YOURS!"

"WHO THE FUCK… TOLD YOU… THAT YOU WERE THE HEAD OF THIS HOUSE!!" Dad yelled back.

Cora was silent.

A few minutes later, I braced when I heard my Dad's heavy steps come up the stairs. I was still sobbing and shaking like a leaf. He never did that before and I was flabbergasted. I got a swift smack on the butt if I got out of line but the beating I just took was out of character. He walked in and knelt by my bed where I lay twitching with pain.

"I'm sorry Shortstuff." He said softly. "I got carried away and I'll never do that again. I was wrong Shorty. I'm sorry."

"It, it's, it's…..ok." I stammered.

"I love you."

"I…..love, love you, too". I said between gasps.

For a while I struggled to catch my breath. Ten minutes later Junior poked his head around the doorway of his room. "HEY, Dad apologized! What else you need?!? Why are you still crying?"

Again I couldn't answer. My ass felt like fire ants were eating it alive. My Dad never laid a hand on me again. He never needed to. I knew what was waiting for me if I ever pissed him off; those big mitts that hung off the end of his arms.

13

Cora was fucking weird. I think she was bipolar. She would go weeks kicking the shit out of me for the smallest things like forgetting to lock the door when I left for school. We lived in a nice neighborhood. It wasn't good ol' suburbia, but it was safe regardless. All the riffraff of mayhem and unrest happened downtown, a full five miles from where we lived. But still, she insisted on me locking the door because I was the last to leave the house and she was left alone still asleep in bed, which I understood completely. She would check the backdoor first thing when she woke up and most times found it unlocked. She would make sure she was waiting in the kitchen when I got home. When I walked through the door, she would commence to smack the shit out of me with no warning.

We used to be a great team when it came to video games. We played the Super Mario Brothers games for years. Every time the newest version came out, Cora or Junior would go buy it and we would all start dissecting them. We were crack addicts for it. Cora and I seemed to play Nintendo non-stop. I was most useful when Dad was drunk, remember?

In 1991 when Nintendo released Super NES, I had cash saved from my birthday a few months earlier. One weekend we were playing Super Mario Brothers 3 on the good old fashioned Nintendo when Cora offered, "You know if you give me your birthday money, I'll kick in the rest and we can get the Super Nintendo and Super Mario World."

That was all I needed to hear. "Sure!" I exclaimed. "Let's get it!"

So we drove down Buffalo Avenue to Williams Road where the Summit Park Mall was, and purchased our game system at a place called Geoffrey's Games and Hobby Shop. We went home, set it up, and reveled in the updated 16-bit video console. It was the latest thing and we loved it. We figured out Super Mario World as we went along. This was 1991 mind you. We didn't have the internet and Google sites with cheat codes and various things to help us out. If you wanted help with a game, you had to buy Nintendo Power Magazine.

We bumbled through it for the first two days but once we figured out what to do, I defeated Bowser and we beat the game in four nights. We were damn proud of ourselves.

So anyway, three, four times a week, after dinner, when Cora didn't hate on me or beat me because the wind was blowing, that was our routine. A few months before the Super Nintendo was released, we were so close to beating Super Mario Brothers 3. We were stuck half way through the eighth and final world for a good three weeks. The boss at the end of the game, for you folks who didn't grow up with the magic that was Super Mario Brothers, is Bowser. He's like this half lizard/dinosaur king that is always kidnapping the princess. *Ain't we all?* The night I finally beat him, I had lost a good dozen lives. My fingers were slipping all over the controller from my clammy hands and finally, SUCCESS! When Princess Toadstool came out at the end and said, 'Thanks for saving me, but the Princess is in another castle', like she did in the original game, we thought we had to play some more. Cora playfully shoved me on the shoulder. *No way, there are more levels!!* But then she realized, it was an inside joke from the Nintendo programmers. We watched the ending credits, because that's your prize of course to see the cool sequence at the end, and then realized it was one-thirty in the morning on a school night. Cora turned to me and said, "Well, you need your rest, so why don't you stay home from school."

To a thirteen year old kid, that is the greatest thing you can say. "Yeah, I am pretty tired."

"Ok then. But you have to stay in the house until school lets out."

"Ok." I agreed. That was just fine by me.

"We had a good run tonight."

"We sure did."

"Ok. Off to bed. Good night Shorty."

"Good night, Cora."

It was little windows like that that were so confusing to me. Cora was a sweet beautiful woman sometimes; a fun woman with passion. It was just so hard to pin down which side of her I was going to get at any given time. So when I woke up the next day, it was no surprise I was being yelled at for having the audacity to stir the air down stairs in her presence.

14

I acquired a Walkman in a trade for some baseball cards from a friend one day. I had asked for one for my previous birthday and, of course, Cora wouldn't let me have one. I started borrowing tapes from Junior and Sonya. Sonya grew to be the quintessential middle wild child. She had a mousy brown volcano of curly hair flowing from her head. She was a real loose cannon with a sharp wit, and *popular* with the boys. She was always coming and going. Sonya was into a lot of different stuff. Her music collection consisted mostly of hair metal bands like Dokken, Cinderella, and Bon Jovi. I loved this stuff. When I went to bed at night I would listen to it very low so I could hear if anyone was coming up the stairs to my room. The hiding spot for this beautiful machine was under my bed. I wasn't allowed in Junior's room so I would sneak in when he wasn't there and make mix tapes of all my favorite bands at the time.

They introduced me to White Lion. Their album 'Pride' saved me from the loneliness of upstairs. The music dissolved the walls of my prison for the short time I was listening. It's funny how a photo or a song can do that. To this day when I hear White Lion, I am immediately thirteen again and that comfort I felt from all the pain comes back.

In school, there was a girl named Michelle. She had curly blonde hair and was on the swim team. She never looked perfect and that's what I liked about her. She liked me as well, but we were young and had no idea how to act. I never had the courage to ask her out because I knew if she said yes, Cora would not let me do anything with her like go to a movie or something. Music like White Lion helped me through that frustration. They wrote songs with haunting guitar riffs and lyrics about lonely nights. "Tell Me" is a song about teenage love and I was going through that agony. Music taught me there is a place inside you that wakes up. Songs will attach to a girl and remind you of that special feeling you felt toward her. Sometimes I hear a White Lion song and think of her. I believe she was the first girl I really liked the way boys do.

15

Cora had this habit of wearing a long shirt as pajamas. There were times I would come down stairs to make myself a bowl of cereal before school and she would be awake doing various things around the house. She had a few shirts that were dangerously short, nothing revealing just short. I never really paid much attention until middle school and hit puberty. I was starting to get acne which we all know sucks big time. She had to know what I was going through. It was a confusing time. I would feel guilty and dirty when I admired her olive skin on her smooth naked legs. My heart would pound out of my chest.

She would make a devious game out of it. I used to sit at the foot of the steps upstairs trying not to make a sound while Cora talked with a friend down stairs in the kitchen. Some days when I eavesdropped like that, it was the only time I heard human voices other that my own. One such conversation I heard her say, *the boys walk around the house in their joggers with their things swinging in their pants like they're king ding-a-ling.*

One morning while I was eating my breakfast, she needed help hanging a picture on the wall and asked me to hold the chair she was using for a stool. As I went to help she stepped up on the chair and said calmly, "Look the other way. I don't want you to see under my shirt." As a horny curious kid I stole a peak at her underwear and admired her butt. The familiar wave of guilt and filth washed over me. I felt there was something wrong with me to want to look up my step mothers' shirt.

One time after school I walked through the door to find a deserted house.

"Hello?" I called out.

"I'm in here." Cora said. Her voice came from the front room where we moved the Nintendo because she didn't want me to have free reign of it upstairs when she sent me there.

I walked through the dining room and popped my head in the door. What I saw stopped me dead in my tracks. She was playing Nintendo, facing the way the television was setup adjacent to the doorway.

She was sitting in the chair wearing only a shirt. It was hiked up on her thighs high enough I could see her white underwear. She pressed pause and the screen shined on her.

I looked up at her eyes. She caught me staring at her crotch.

"How was school?" She asked.

My heart was pounding in my ears. "Good." I squeaked out.

"You wanna play Nintendo?" *Nen-tendo.* "I need help with this level?" She asked. She slightly leaned back in the chair and spread her legs. The movements made me look back, and I could see that her panties were old and washed to the point they were transparent. I could see her pubic hair and everything she had in perfect detail. The guilt hit me again. To my horror I felt my penis start to throb.

"Um, ok. I'll be right back." I said and walked away. By the time I ran up the stairs and was barely past the landing, I was raging hard. I ripped it out of my pants and masturbated. After about twenty seconds, I leaned with my back against the wall, wallowing in my guilt for what I had just done. Nausea punched me in the face. *Don't throw up, don't throw up, don't throw up...* I thought.

I couldn't hold it. My stomach clenched hard, I doubled over, and retched a long hard gag until a teaspoon of burning stomach acid came up and dripped to the carpet. My stomach lurched again and my body did a hybrid half machine gun burp, half gag thing. My mouth hung open and rained saliva. I retched again but nothing came out. The sound of me gasping for breath echoed through the upstairs. I retched one last long hard gag and spit on the floor and the nausea faded away. On my hands and knees it was then I realized during the ordeal my colon had unleashed a king sized pile in my pants.

I got off my knees, peeled off my shirt, and scrubbed the semen and stomach acid off of the carpet. I peeled off my underwear, shit and all, stuck it in my little garbage can, and tied up the bag to hide it under my bed until I threw it in trash can outside the next morning. I turned the shower on and got under the stream to wash off the stench. I noticed I was still erect. I stared at it for a few seconds.

"Fuck it." I said, and masturbated again fantasizing about Cora's half covered vagina that was now vividly burned into my brain. Twenty seconds later the deed was done. I sat down in the tub with the water pouring over me and started to cry.

After a while she stopped walking around like that. She probably figured I was going through some changes, and was more cautious. I don't know. I would have CRAZY dreams about Cora. A few times I dreamt that I was getting a blow job from a beautiful girl. I would look down and see Cora looking back up at me. I would wake up in a cold sweat with a mess in my underwear. A few other times, I would be having sex with a dreamy girl. Then she would turn over on her back, revealing a fantastic set of breasts. I would look at her face and she would be Cora. *Cold sweats.* I started having stomach issues. It was upset and nauseous most of the time because of the anguish I felt for having graphic sexual dreams and fantasies of her.

16

I wasn't the only one getting the blunt end of Cora's abuse. For years there was a tug of war between Cora and Junior. Big difference here, when Cora showed up, Junior was ten. By the time he was in high school, he could defend himself against her. She hadn't sunk into his armor like she did mine. I was young, in need of a mother and very impressionable—a recipe for disaster.

Junior dated a girl named Kate his senior year. She was a nice all-American girl complete with a ponytail that bobbed with her stride. She thought I was adorable and included me in her dates with Junior from time to time. Junior was cool enough to let me tag along. The three of us went shopping once and she bought me a Minnesota North Stars t-shirt because she knew I was a big fan of Mike Modano. Another time she baked sugar cookies for Junior and made a separate batch for me. That was really cool. Cora thought Kate was controlling Junior. Truth was, Junior just wanted to get away from Cora. Whenever Kate called the house, he disappeared for the night. I liked her because she pissed Cora off something awful.

One night at dinner the phone rang. Cora looked over to Junior, clapped once and exclaimed, "Oh, interception! She won't give you the time of day, will she?"

On his way to answer, Junior shot her a glare that burned through her skull. He was rolling his head on his shoulders like a boxer getting ready to fight. His ears burned a fiery red. He spoke into the phone to Kate for a few minutes making plans for their night. Nights like this, I tried so hard to stay awake until Junior came home at eleven o'clock. I felt safer when he came home for the night. I felt like I was protected from the monster down stairs.

Cora was doing laundry one Saturday and somehow pissed off Junior with one of her snide comments about Kate. He started yelling back at her and Cora threw Junior's clothes out the back door. Junior followed after, picked up the clothes furiously, slung open the door and slammed the clothes in a laundry basket where they both started tugging. They yelled at each other until finally Junior yanked the basket away from Cora and slammed it to the ground. Junior stormed out and met Dad in the garage. Of course I was banished to the upstairs while this was all going on. Through the upstairs kitchen window I could see the back yard and the garage quite well. Of course I eavesdropped on what was going on in the garage when I heard Junior yell, "GET HER AWAY FROM ME BEFORE I KILL HER!!"

"Who, Sonya?!?" Dad asked. Sonya was over innocently visiting with Cora when this incident broke out. She was in the kitchen frozen with confusion wondering how to take this recent turn of events. Dad came through the door and realized it was Cora who Junior wanted to kill and immediately started to defuse the situation. "Go for a walk, Partner." He said.

I knew something was going to break, and FAST. Cora was always talking to me about Junior. *That brother of yours is such a lame brain. He isn't going to amount to jack shit.* She also called me a lame brain that more times than I could count. That was her favorite name she liked to call Junior and I.

I wasn't allowed to leave the two block radius around my house. Sixty-fifth and sixty-sixth streets in Niagara Falls are sandwiched in between the Interstate 190 and the LaSalle Expressway. But the expressway had a nice walkway bridge over it. So I would ride my bike over that thing and for years I was scared to go further in fear that I wouldn't hear my Dad call for me to come home. The summer between eighth and ninth grades, little by little, I would ride further and further. Pretty soon I was riding all over uptown; LaSalle it was called. All the way to the mall on Williams Road, a good distance away. This was ballsy for me, the kid scared shitless of Cora finding out about my new adventures.

One day, riding my bike I ran into a few friends of mine. Charlie and Phil Simpson where born nine months apart in consecutive years and were in the same grade as me. I had met them the previous school year. They were typical all-American kids that beat up on each other every chance they could like brothers do. They could have passed for twins. Charlie was lanky with a New Yorkers sharp tongue, and Phil outweighed him by twenty pounds and was as calm as a priest on Sunday. Other than that, their mannerisms were a spot on match and they loved to beat each other up. They punched each other all the time like a running joke.

They were real cool cats. They signed up through Columbia House, which was an album distribution company in the nineties, and bought all these CD's. When they bought a CD to upgrade from the cassette tape, they would give the tape to me. This was the time I was introduced to bands like Iron Maiden, Metallica, and Pink Floyd.

The Simpson Brothers were friends with a kid named Barney Lombardo. Barney was a small wiry Italian kid who wore thin black framed glasses, had a sharp wit, and was gritty. I liked him immediately. He had similar taste in music and girls as I did. He had a go-cart we all used to blast around his neighborhood and piss off the neighbors.

One day I rode my bike to Charlie and Phil's house on a hot July morning. Charlie said, "We're meeting Barney over at Joe Park. We're gonna ride the go-cart there."

I was confused. "I though he blew the motor on it?" I said.

"Yeah, he did. But he took it off so we're gonna push it up the hill then ride it down."

"Sounds a bit weird but I'm down with that. Is he fixing it like he said he was gonna?"

"I don't know anymore," Phil said, "he changes his mind every fifteen minutes." Phil smacked Charlie on the back of his neck. Charlie returned with a knee jerk reaction punch to Phil's chest that made him exhale with an, *Ooot!* Phil unsuccessfully tried to trip Charlie.

"Your MOTHER!" Charlie shouted.

"Shitface." Phil returned.

Joe Park was in the nice section of town five blocks away. There was three nice baseball diamonds the city's youth little leagues used every year and a big jungle gym at the East end of the park for small children. At the West end past the ball diamonds was a hill about fifteen feet tall with a grade between fifteen degrees at the bottom and a steeper thirty at the top.

Charlie, Phil, and I arrived at the park to find Barney on top of the hill with his go-cart. The jalopy screamed down, and at the end Barney swung the back axle of the cart around and skidded to a halt. It looked like a blast. We ran over to him and marveled at the genius of his *newly designed* go-cart. I thought it was a brilliant idea at the time. For a few hours we took turns gunning down the hill looking like a group of wild hoodlums in a stolen car. Then someone suggested that for extra weight, we should have two people ride the back. The cart will go faster. Brilliant plan!

When the motor blew a few weeks prior, Barney took the whole unit off which was located behind the seat. This left an open space where there was only a skeleton frame the motor once was. To have two people ride on the back for extra weight, you have one guy stand on the frame to the left, one on the right. The frame metal was made of angle iron, so you had to put your right foot on top of your left foot because you only had a few inches of metal to stand on, and hold the back of the seat with your hands. The other guy stood the same on the right frame rail shoulder to shoulder to each other.

This particular run Barney was driving the cart with Phil and me on the back. I was on the left. We did this a dozen times that day. We started down the hill and halfway down Barney was setting up his skid. First, he turned the wheel right then left to skid out the back end. This time was different. Barney turned right and it caught us off guard. Phil immediately jumped off the cart. I went to follow suit but I lost footing and I fell backward. My right foot caught on something and Barney dragged me down the hill.

When Barney removed the motor, it left the chain sprocket on the frame which was about four to six inches from the back of the seat. My foot had caught between the seat and the sprocket. I got up and told Barney to roll back the go-cart so I can remove my foot. I started walking it off feeling pretty lucky I didn't break my leg or ankle. I heard joints in my foot crack and pop like popcorn. I was immediately glad I didn't feel any pain as I paced a few laps.

"Shit man, are you ok?!?" Barney exclaimed.

"Man that was a close one." I said as I paced. "That was a FUCKIN close one. That could have been worse."

From a few yards behind me where he had jumped off, Phil turned white as a ghost. "Shorty, don't look down." He said calmly.

"Why? What are you talk…?" In mid-sentence I looked down at my sneaker.

When my right foot was caught, it wedged pointing right with the seat against the arch side and the sprocket on the outside. The sprocket had sawed through my high top sneaker, my sock, and finally the skin. The gash in my ankle started just above my heal bone, up in the thin skin between the Achilles' tendon and that knob bone at the outside of your foot, and a little past about four and a half inches long. My skin had stretched open about two inches so when I looked down I saw a dark oval hole in my foot and clean red muscle like in a biology book.

I immediately fell to the ground and started howling. It didn't hurt. I was just in shock of what I just saw. Phil took off my sawed up sneaker and sock. He then stuck my sock on the wound and I started to scream.

"AAAAHHHHH!!! What are you doing?" I yelled at him.

He calmly said, "I'm applying direct pressure."

"FUCK!" I yelped. The pain blasted me. My ankle screamed at me until my endorphins kicked in. A few minutes later a woman in her early twenties came over and said, "I saw the whole thing! I called 911. An ambulance is on the way." She had curly blond hair and wore a green two piece bikini. She had been sun bathing in her yard when this event unfolded in front of her like a bad movie. She knelt by me and said, "Its ok sweetie. Help is coming." She stayed there the entire time. Phil had gotten up and was standing with Barney about six feet away from us. While I was on the ground, I heard the ambulance siren in the distance getting stronger.

Despite the commotion and noise, I heard Barney quietly say clear as day, "Hey Phil, check out the tits on that chick." I'm sure Blondie heard it. But she was classy enough not to call him out. Someone must have called Dad and Cora because they arrived out of nowhere. They looked visibly shaken. They followed the ambulance to the hospital. I knew I was in deep shit then. Cora made it a point to say in my ear that *we weren't going to talk about it now, but you're grounded indefinitely for being so far from home and for scaring the shit out of me and your father.*

I have a fine looking scar from that little incident. I ended up with fourteen staples and multiple stitches to repair the little cut in my leg muscle. If my foot had slipped in pointing left instead of right, the sprocket would have cut through my Achilles and snapped it like a thread. I would have what they call a *pimpin walk* today. I was very lucky.

We hung out all that summer and the next. Charlie grew up to be a renowned chef who cooks for corporate bigwigs and celebrities. Phil, unfortunately, had a string of bad luck with drugs in his twenties and later died of a stroke in his thirties.

17

One night, the storm got a bit darker when our two cousins from the Air Force came over to talk to Junior because he was thinking about joining the military. Junior had blown out his knee in his junior year so his football career took a major hit. College recruiters tend to get cold feet after a wide receiver gets a bum knee. He still had offers from Division II schools but nothing like before his injury.

Dad called them over to hang out and have a few totties. They talked about how cool it was and divulged in the debauchery they got into with buddies they met from around the world. They were Gulf War veterans. They talked of their tours over in Iraq and Kuwait. That was a cool night. We hadn't seen much of them growing up because they were a few years older than Junior and I. So it was nice when they came to visit.

Junior was hooked and quickly signed up not long after that. Dad and Cora decided I could have Junior's room when he left. So I was excited to have a bigger room and the whole upstairs apartment to myself. I was sad to see him go. The night before he left, he was going to bed early because he had to be in Buffalo at the crack of dawn. He turned off his bedroom light and stuck his head out the door at me.

"I'm sorry I have to do this Shorty." He said. "I'm sorry I'm not going to be here to protect you from Cora. But it will be over soon. Hang in there."

"It's ok. At least I'm getting your room."

That made him laugh, it had been a while. Then he said serious as a judge, "I have to do this or I'll kill her, you understand?"

"Yeah."

"When I get set up, I'll let you know so you can call me anytime ok?"

"Ok."

"Just don't do anything stupid, ok? Dad is right. Your time is coming."

"It's all good."

The next morning he said a heart felt goodbye to me before he left. He gave an emotionless half hug to Cora without saying a word to her and went out the back door to the garage after Dad.

And just like that, I was left alone to fend for myself.

18

Sonya came over to the house for a visit after "The Go-cart Incident" as it came to be known. She dredged upstairs and we had a heart to heart about Cora treating me like shit and banishing me to the dungeon. She gave me some books from her collection because she knew I was grounded for a good while. She gave me "When We Dead Awaken" by John R. Holt, which is an AWESOME book. She also gave me "Four Past Midnight", and "The Bachman Books" by Stephen King. Those stories got me through the dungeon. His stories were dark and creepy, which was unfortunately my life at that moment. I liked them because they resonated with me. I wanted to be in these stories; to escape. They kept my sanity, which by that time was dripping away slowly like a seeping oil pan.

After a few months there was light at the end of the tunnel, and Sonya had told me that when I was no longer grounded, I could hang out with her at her apartment down town about forty blocks away. That was a hop, skip, and a jump for me on the bike. When she told me that, I was elated.

The day I was no longer grounded, it was early winter so I was stuck upstairs regardless because my Sixty-fifth Street buddies were no longer hanging around the neighborhood and I was left behind. No one wants to hang out with a kid who was not allowed to do anything anyway.

So I just stayed home to stay warm from the harsh winter of Western New York. I couldn't ride to Sonya's in the snow, so that plan died until spring.

But Sonya reminded me every time she came over to visit. When the snow melted, I called her collect, and made the ride down. Her apartment was a small one bedroom that had water stains and chipping paint on the ceiling. The kitchenette had linoleum flooring from the seventies and it showed its wear. She had MTV, so we would hang out and watch music videos. One day she gave me a tape of the album "Dirt" by Alice in Chains. That changed my life. Since I started listening to tapes on my Walkman, it was my get away. Even now when I hear any song from that record I am immediately fifteen again and hanging out at her old apartment. The songs are so dark and brooding and the chords in the songs are mostly minor. At night I would pull out the Walkman and listen to these tapes. They took me away to where Cora was not. I was safe in this world. It was my world, a place just for me. This was the grunge era, so bands like Nirvana, Pearl Jam, Sponge, and Soundgarden kept me safe. The guys in these bands were my friends. But not like Alice in Chains. I lived through that band. If I was depressed for any reason, or if Cora kicked the shit out of me, that band was my go to escape.

Grandpa would drive down to Punxsutawney, Pennsylvania every summer and I always tagged along. I couldn't wait to go all year. The trip would get me away from Cora. My mother's side of the family had roots there and Grandpa would hunt on their property that was deep in the mountains. His sister had a rickety shack she lived in just on the edge of the woods. I loved that place because it was so quiet being so far away from town. There was a church and a cemetery across the road that creeped me out something fierce. But Stephen King helped me get over that. Grandpa without fail would tag a few deer and bring home a few dozen pounds of venison, so when I came over his house after our Sunday pancake breakfasts, he would make venison stew for us, which was to die for. I thoroughly enjoyed those trips.

This last trip was a long weekend and we got back to Niagara Falls on Monday morning. Dad had taken the day off to repair and clean the gutters which *had trees growing from them* as he put it. I yapped about our trip to Dad and Cora until Grandpa decided to go home. Cora was especially sweet that morning. She even hugged me and said she missed me, which was weird to say the least. After Grandpa left I went upstairs to my bedroom because I had conceded to the idea of being up there all day, and to unpack my things.

I noticed my room was cleaned. On the opposite wall, Cora's stereo was set up in my room. This thing if I even breathed on it wrong, she would knock me into next week. Every unit in the cabinet was shiny and silver like polished aluminum. It was a nice system. The receiver was made by Technics as well as the cassette player. The record player was a Sony with a glass cover and new needles. Now I didn't have to sneak down stairs when Cora and Dad weren't home to listen to her Asia record. It had internal lights that shined through the tuner dial and face plate. The speaker cabinets held twelve inch woofers with tweeters that sounded like magic. I loved having that thing on at night. It soothed me after years of having an over active imagination that sometimes kept me awake past midnight. Also, because

I was afraid of the dark and the light was a perfect illumination when I was trying to sleep.

I ran down stairs. Cora and Dad were watching television at the breakfast bar. "I can't believe it!" I exclaimed. "Why is your stereo in my room?" I asked Cora.

"Well I don't listen to it anymore so I thought you would get use out of it. Will you take care of it for me?"

"Sure! I'll make sure it stays nice, and I will take VERY good care of it."

She smiled at me. It was one of the few times of all the years I knew her that she genuinely smiled at me, and she hugged me again. I remember it felt fantastic. I ran upstairs and threw in my Pink Floyd "The Wall" cassette. It sounded GREAT. I was so excited and confused at the same time. Never in my wildest dreams did I think Cora would do such a thing. This is the woman that kicked the shit out of me for the smallest thing, purposely teased, and berated me. But who was I to question. She was being nice for a change and when she was in these moods, I enjoyed it.

19

"Let's go for a ride Shorty." Dad said as he languidly walked through the back door to the laundry room. Cora followed with her head down gazing the floor. They looked dejected. Past experience told me bad news was coming when he asked me to *go for a ride*.

"Ok. Where are we going?"

"Nowhere, just around." He mustered.

"Ok."

I slipped into my sneakers and waited by the back

door. Dad was fumbling around for his keys. Cora had taken off her coat and hung it on the rack in the hall between the kitchen and laundry room when she came in. She looked back at me and disappeared into the house. Dad realized his keys were in his pocket then said, "Let's go."

This isn't good. I thought. *He is too quiet and Cora is anxious about something. Maybe they're divorcing. Good fucking riddance Bitch! Sure, the stereo was a nice gesture, but years of torture are hard for me to forgive. It wasn't good to know ya! I'll miss you never!*

We walked out to the garage. Dad had a Black Ford Ranger at the time that he regularly waxed. It gleamed and I could see my reflection in the finish despite the weather, which was overcast and chilly. He took really good care of his vehicles. We backed down the driveway and into the street. He put the Ranger in drive and said, "Cora has a brain tumor, and it's malignant."

My jaw dropped open. For years I wished this woman dead and now she had cancer. A huge wave of guilt washed over me and I immediately thought it was my fault. I actually wished this on her. I felt about three inches tall.

"Is she going to be ok?" I asked.

"We don't know. The doctors don't know how long she's had it. A few weeks ago she started having sudden bad headaches for a minute or two."

"Is that where you were coming from just now?"

"Yeah." There was a cancer hospital in Buffalo; one of the best in the nation.

"So…"

"She's going to be fine." He interrupted. "She's going to have brain surgery and then start chemo. You don't have to do anything special. Just carry on like any other day ok?"

"Ok."

"We're tough. We can handle this. We pull up our socks and keep going. It's what we do." He said as he stared out the windshield. "Basic 101."

I was still in shock from the guilt. We drove around the city for about a half hour in silence. It was all a blur. The guilt numbed me.

Cora was sitting in her recliner watching television when we arrived back at the house. I felt weird so I went upstairs to listen to music. *I wish she was dead* echoed through my brain like bad feedback. This was surreal. I never knew anyone with cancer. The guilt piled on and felt as heavy as concrete.

20

That summer while "The Lion King" was smashing records at the box office, Cora had her surgery and it was a success. There was a good twenty percent of the tumor left in her brain but the doctors said there was a decent chance that radiation and chemo would take care of the rest. Her hair fell out, so she wore huge hoop earrings to offset her shinny head in public. She was fighting valiantly. The Air Force had stationed Junior in Grand Forks, North Dakota working on missile silos. When he came back to visit, Cora apologized to him for being so difficult all these years; *a pain in the keister,* she put it. Her Doctor said he didn't know how long she had the tumor. She told Junior maybe that was the cause of all her outbursts. Junior accepted and she was sweet as pie after that.

Things got easier around the house. She was joking more and Dad was around. I mean, he was THERE. It was good. Things at home were GOOD. We played Nintendo again. She cooked again. She was making her mean spaghetti sauce homemade from scratch, and showed me how to make it. She was doing that all the time. She was a fantastic cook of course because of her Italian heritage, so she was making all sorts of dishes again. She even made some that she didn't before like homemade gnocchi, manicotti, braccioli, polenta, and ravioli. Good lord, I forgot how awesome of a cook she was and she reminded me every night at the dinner table. She took interest in what was going on in my life. When Dad had to work overtime, we would go out to dinner just the two of us and talk about school, and movies, and books, and music we both liked. She was again the mother I never had. We would sit at the breakfast bar and listen to songs on the kitchen radio like, "The Captain of her Heart" by Double. She would tell me memories that were connected to certain songs that played, and reminisced about spending her early twenties in California.

That lasted three months. And frankly, it was the best three months I had ever spent with Cora. I look back at that time fondly. My father was fun, Cora was fun, and LIFE was fun. Until little by little, the real Cora came back. And Dad camped out on the couch again. I was back in the dungeon. I had tasted the good life, and it was good while it lasted.

21

Eleventh grade was a little better for me. It didn't

start out that way though. I had applied for a job at McDonalds, *McAmerica*, and they hired me. It was my very first job and I finally had some jingle in my pockets. I constantly volunteered to close the store because the few people that closed with me I liked. As a bonus, my manager though I was cool and gave me the easy jobs. There was a girl that loved to crank the album "Core" by Stone Temple Pilots after hours. I loved it there. It was a safe haven. So when school started back up, because of New York State labor laws, it was bye-bye closing shifts during the week and hello to shitty nights at home with a lunatic stepmother and absentee father. Julia Reynolds, a girl I knew from school, also worked at McDonalds. I heard around the campfire she was *easy*. She was a short thin girl with medium length brown hair and a cute smile with full kissable lips. On a slow night at work we were all sitting around shooting the breeze as we did those nights, and she was hinting to me she had no one to go with to Homecoming. So I worked up the courage to ask her, and she said yes. It was crummy of me to ask her in hopes of getting my dick wet. Junior was in the habit of asking me every time he called home so it was the only thing on my brain.

> *"So Shorty, you get laid yet?"*
> *"No. Not even close."*
> *"Are you gay? Cause it's ok if you are."*
> *"No course not. I like girls. I just haven't found a girlfriend yet."*

That made its way into our last few conversations. So I was stoked a few weeks after I asked her to homecoming we started hanging out. We would hang out at her house after work and make out on her couch until she would send me home with a hard on the size of Texas. Sex was all of a sudden the ONLY thing on my mind. Of course it was, I was sixteen.

That year I enrolled in an accelerated math course because math is one of my loves. The teacher for the class was a real cool cat. He was a tall thick man with a hair style like Einstein. He used to play saxophone and guitar for various local blues bands around the Buffalo area. His street cred was substantial in my book. He would pick me to go work problems on the blackboard in front of the class because he would notice I was paying more attention to the ladies in class than the derivatives he was teaching. He would call me names by the band shirt I wore. If I wore my Nine Inch Nails shirt, he called me Nin Boy, and if I wore my R.E.M. shirt, I was Rem that day. I didn't mind, he was a fun dude. He had good intentions.

"Hey Rem, What the freq, Ken?"

That is what was on the back of my R.E.M. shirt; lyrics. "Sorry." I said, busted again talking to the girl in the next aisle.

"Go to the board. I have a derivative with your name on it."

"Ugh." I trudged to the front of the class. There were girls paying attention to me and I was starting to like it. The more I was called out, the more they paid attention.

One day I got a tap on my shoulder from the kid behind me. I turned around and he gave me a note. Inside it read,

Hey, I'm Miriam. We take gym together. Are you taking anyone to Homecoming? If not, I was

wondering if you wanted to go with me???

I looked back at her. We sat in the first column of desks by the door. She sat in the back row three rows behind where I sat. I wrote,

Miriam,
Sorry I have a girlfriend.

I folded up the note as best I could and gave it back to the kid behind me. The two kids between us passed off the note to Miriam smooth like they rehearsed it. Grab and pass over shoulder, grab and pass over shoulder. A few minutes later I hear a pounding behind me. I looked back and Miriam's lightly banging her head on the desk. A few girls around the classroom started snickering at her. If I was single I would have said yes. Why wouldn't I? She was about 5'3" and a hundred pounds soaking wet. She had medium length blond curly hair with brown streaks, blue eyes the shade of the sky, and a smile that shined. She would find a date within the week.

22

The Wednesday before homecoming, I had to tell Julia I couldn't go. I didn't have the money to pay for my end of the limousine and I couldn't get off work. She said it was ok and not to worry about it. But the following Monday at school, she tracked me down in the hall and gave me the—we need to talk—conversation at my locker. After it was all said and done, I was dumped.

Junior year looked like it was going to be like the last two years. But I was used to being a loner. What's another year or two? *I'm going to be a virgin forever.* I remember thinking. *Now it's back to the dungeon at home.* But I was wrong.

After Miriam and I passed that note in math class, we started talking in gym. We had a nice laugh when she told me why she was banging her head on her desk. Apparently I was the fifth or sixth guy she asked that week and turned her down for various reasons. We started passing notes in class through the network of kids in our aisle. Grab and pass over shoulder, grab and pass over shoulder. Miriam Roberson was adorable. She was the most beautiful girl I had ever seen to that point in my life and she was as sweet as apple pie. I quickly forgot about Julia when I asked Miriam out to a movie. "Interview with the Vampire" was playing that weekend and I read the book by Anne Rice a few years back while exiled to the dungeon.

So, that night in November, Miriam and I with another couple trudged three or four miles to the Junction Summit Movie Complex where we met some other classmate couples and various people Miriam knew from class. Miriam's rat pack of buddies was the same giggling hens that were snickering at her in class the day she asked me to Homecoming. They were all sophomores. I didn't mind hanging out with these kids. At least I had more friends to hang out with, younger than me or not.

The movie was better than the book. I was the only one of the pack that had read it. It is still one of my favorite movies. That night was a good date. We talked about music and movies we liked, and after the movie, we talked about favorite TV shows. Her favorite was a relatively unknown show that just debuted and was slowly gaining popularity among the kids at our school. That show was called "Friends." When we got back to her house, we made out for a while. I felt like a bad ass kissing this smoking hot blonde.

Things didn't stay that way though. Miriam was prude so she was no good to me. I was so stupid and relentless. Her friend Amanda was single and I found out that she previously had sex with a prior boyfriend. One night everyone went ice skating without me. Amanda who had a crush on me told me Miriam was a little friendlier than she should have been with some other cat. So I dumped her and started dating Amanda. That was Amanda's plan from the start. This turned out to be a massive error in judgment. I would spend years trying to get Miriam back.

Amanda had a nice look to her. She had dark straight hair and a slight year round tan because she was one-quarter Native American. She had curves in all the right places. She was shy when she was around people she didn't know, but with her friends she was the typical extrovert Yankee.

We already hung out a few times before we started dating so I knew she was nice. I took her to this happening bar and grill called Sweet Stones in Donald Junction on our first date. It had all these microbrews on tap and was the first of its kind to feature such before it was cool and trendy. We couldn't drink any of course, but there was a shelf in the back that held movie scripts that local talent had written. Art works of locals hung on the walls. There were wine tastings on the weekends and their menu consisted of gourmet sandwiches. Amanda and I sat with our sandwiches and talked of our favorite movies. Miriam came up in the conversation and we talked about how prude she was. Amanda made it a point to tell me she wasn't. I felt a warm feeling south of my belt when I heard her say that and fantasized about what she looked like naked for the rest of the night.

Four days into our relationship, she invited me over to her house. It was an old brick structure built in the early 1900's. It contained four bedrooms, three bathrooms, and a monster attic space. There were laundry shoots in each room where the clothes would converge down in the old stone basement. The fireplace in the living room was framed with gorgeous carved trim that continued around the room.

She gave me a hug when I arrived and led me upstairs to her room. She was wearing a baggy red Forty-Niners sweat shirt and snug jean shorts. I watched her sway her hips ahead of me and I recalled the conversation we had about her not being prude like Miriam. In her room was a waterbed. It was firm, but had just enough motion in it.

"Wow, that's cool." I said pointing to the waterbed. "I never knew anyone with one. I've seen them in movies but never in real life."

"They're nice." She answered. "Especially on cold winter nights like last night." She sat on it and pawed at a dial that was protruding from the rail. "See? It's heated."

"Sweet, this thing is awesome." I commented. I sat down next to her. Her bare tan legs looked smooth as silk. By the bed was a rack full of CD's. I knelt in front of it like a church pew. "What do we have here? Who are you into?"

"Hmm, the usual stuff. Aerosmith, Guns N' Roses, Gin Blossoms."

I grabbed a Soul Asylum CD. "Grave Dancers Union… This isn't bad. Not my taste, but if it was on the radio I wouldn't turn it off."

"Man, its warm in here," she said and pulled her sweater over her head, "that's better."

Her dark hair sprawled on her shoulder. She gave it a quick rustle and a flip and her hair fell behind her. Her blood red lacy bra bled through her white Aerosmith concert shirt.

Holy shit that's a nice rack! I thought. The familiar warm feeling south of my belt came back. "I like Black Gold. That's a cool jam."

"Yeah, it's ok. I'm more into the Gin Blossoms now." Amanda said.

"Well, they're not my cup of tea. But at least you don't have any Richard Marx CD's I can see."

Amanda stood up and laughed. "Yeah, he sucks. Miriam loves him. He's like her favorite singer."

"Her whole taste in music was lame to be honest." I added.

"There's a lot of things lame about her, that prude."

"She was. I left her house horny as a dog more than once. I think she got off on turning me down."

"Sex feels too good. She doesn't know what she's missing. She's a virgin you know." She looked away from me and stared at the floor. "I… wouldn't do that to you."

My jeans were getting incredibly tight. I saw her erect nipples under the fabric of her shirt. My senses ignited because I never saw that in the flesh; only in movies but this was much better.

Amanda stood in front of me. Her forehead was starting to shine with a faint mist of perspiration from her heightened pulse. I was frozen. I was reading her signals but I didn't know what to do. I just knew I wanted her so bad. She looked at the bulge in my pants and stepped closer to me. She was so close I felt her warm breath on my throat. She smelled of sweet apple lotion. "I won't do that to you." She said softly.

I leaned in and kissed her. I felt her warm breasts press against me. She kissed me back.

Of course being sixteen and this being my first sexual experience, I lasted about three and a half minutes and Amanda was left unsatisfied. I felt like a rock star.

On the walk back to my house, I remember reaching my hands to the sky and embracing the snow. The flakes fell in chunks as big as golf balls, floating, slowly and serenely to the ground. It accumulated on the trees making them look like big white paint brushes with sprawled out bristles. The smell of the snow and winter in the air was epic. The atmosphere was soft and quiet that night. I felt like a man; a lord of all creation filled with excitement and wonder. That's what I felt the night I lost my virginity to Amanda Kurtz.

Amanda and I had a routine for a while. Go to the movies, rent movies, and fuck. That's all we did. We would go out to dinner every now and again, but that was it. I forgot the condoms one night and Amanda let me have sex with her anyway. That was a whole new euphoria, but we were a special kind of stupid for starting that habit. That got old quick. A sixteen year old boy wants two things, sex and more sex. Amanda wanted a nice boy and a nice relationship. She talked of marriage and what we would name our kids. I never paid any attention to her. I didn't want any of that. So our relationship was rocky from the start. I only saw Amanda as a safe haven from Cora.

23

One night, I asked Dad and Cora if I could have a later curfew. My brother was allowed to stay out to ten-thirty, eleven when he was a junior. I just wanted the same curfew as my friends. Also, I wanted more time with Amanda; more time, more sex. I was a good kid and up to that point and I never got into any trouble—unless you counted the Joe Park incident—because I was scared shitless by Cora. Of course Cora shot me down and Dad didn't contest her. Maybe he just didn't have the strength to. After that conversation I decided I had enough. I took it upon myself and made a decision to stay the night at Amanda's on the upcoming Friday night. I was done. I couldn't take Cora's shit anymore. Did I overreact? Sure, but I would have killed her if I stayed. I understood what Junior talked about the night he left for the Air Force. I was at that point.

Friday came, Amanda and I decided to watch a movie with her younger sister and sister's friend. We chatted around a bowl of tortilla chips and salsa while watching Amanda's jumpy copy of "The Breakfast Club" on VHS. At eleven-thirty, Cora knocked at Amanda's front door. I walked to the foyer and saw her silhouette through the door drapes. *FUCK!* I thought. *How'd she know I was here? They were supposed to find out when I strolled back home in the morning.* Dejected, I let her in.

"Get in the car. You're coming with me." She was serious as a heart attack.

I looked back at Amanda. She knew full well about my little plan. She helped with it. "I'll see you tomorrow."

"No you won't." Cora added.

Before I closed the door behind me I gave Amanda a little wink. *Oh, yes I will.*

The car was silent most of the drive home until Cora piped up and said, "We'll talk about this in the morning." *Yeah, we sure will talk about this in the morning.* I thought.

That night I couldn't sleep. I was done living in the dungeon. I'd rather live under a bridge. I've spent so long lamenting the ghost of my mother here and enduring Cora's abuse. My head was full and about to burst.

I was up early shoving clothes in a plastic garbage bag the next morning. I trudged down the stairs to tell Dad and Cora I could no longer live there. The kitchen smelled of toast. Dad told me to be careful. Cora said I would be back. I told her I would, to pick up the rest of my things when I find a place. Then out the door I went. I was sixteen and on my own traipsing down the street with a garbage bag full of underwear. That afternoon Amanda and I asked her Mom if I could stay with them. At first she agreed. I paid thirty dollars a week to help out. But that lasted only three weeks. I think her Mom thought initially she would be ok with the prospect of me having sex with her daughter under her roof but decided otherwise and told me to leave. It's completely understandable looking back on it now. Amanda was devastated. She had proudly set up a spare room for me. Her favorite thing to do was to sneak in after her Mom and sister had gone to bed, have a quiet quickie with me and sneak off back to her room.

After that, there was no way I was going back home

so I asked my friend Mack if I could crash on his couch. Our fathers are best friends so we were by default. Growing up, we saw each other on all the major holidays and were invited to all family birthday parties. When Cora was diagnosed with cancer we started hanging out more. His father knew what was going on but never said a word to us. But I knew after a few days my welcome was over stayed so I told Mack a story about moving in with some chick I was banging. I was reduced to sleeping under the overpass of the Grand Island Bridge. It was late winter and still cold so I didn't sleep much. It was dangerous because if a cop spotted me, they would take me home. *I'd rather shoot myself in the face than go home.* I would steal a shower from Mack's house a few times a week too, and as an added bonus he would throw a few of my shirts in the wash. That got old quick because I never had clean clothes. My clothes were scattered between Amanda's house and Mack's. Sonya caught wind of my situation and let me stay at her house for a few days and convinced me to ask my Grandpa if I could stay with him. He lived in a bad section of town but all I wanted was a roof over my head.

I moved in and set up the last of my worldly possessions in the attic. I still had a few albums and a nice radio to listen to so I was happy. That turned out to be a great time, other than Grandpa being a Yankees fan. Whenever they were on television in the afternoon we would watch. Sometimes in silence, other times I would make small talk filling him in about things going on at school or Cora's remission. It was a great time of peace for me. Napping on his couch while the game was playing was a little slice of heaven I will never forget.

24

By the time the air was getting warmer and giving way to summer, I heard word around the campfire that Cora's cancer returned. Little tumors had started to pop up everywhere in her brain so she started more chemotherapy and radiation. I was conflicted. There were so many different thoughts and emotions in my head. I thought I would explode at any moment. Ever since Mack and I started hanging out more frequently, I noticed he had become quite the educated kid when it came to recreational drugs. He established quite a sweet hookup through a cousin of his. He introduced me to the wonders of marijuana. He had a constant supply of weed and alcohol so I was heavily medicating myself to forget everything going on around me.

A favorite ritual of ours was to score some Jamaican red hair and go back to my Grandpa's place. It was the greatest thing ever. I remember the first time the weed bit into my brain. The hazy fog that covers you that first time, it's like getting laid. We would then commence to get high and giggle like two hyenas until we awoke Grandpa accidentally, and he would let us know in a few select broken words to shut the fuck up or else. This went on for months. We had become night owls when school had let out for summer. I would stay up for days only catching cat naps here and there on Mack's couch when we were uptown a few miles walk from Grandpas apartment.

One night in July after a weeklong bender with Mack, I was sleeping off the day at Grandpas. I got there around ten in the morning. I had taken a much needed hot shower and planned to sleep until the nightfall, then meet up with Mack to discuss our *plan of attack* for the night.

When I crawled into my bed there was some weed left over in the cubby of my headboard. So I rolled the rest of it in a fat joint, smoked it and floated off to sleep.

When I awoke, the sun was gone and the street lights were shining their familiar beams of light through the blinds in the window casting strips of shadows over me on the bed. I had wondered if I had slept through the whole next day to the next night. It was quite a regular thing for Mack and me to party for days on end at a friend's house with covered windows and to emerge in the daylight not knowing what day it was or not realizing how many days had passed. A warm breeze from the day's heat was lightly blowing in the window and it felt heavenly. I was still disoriented and did not realize my phone was ringing. I looked at my alarm clock that sat on the night stand. The red digital numbers had read 10:31. I figured it was Mack. I reached out and fumbled with the receiver.

"Hello?"

"Shorty..." It was Junior.

"Yeah…"

"Cora died."

"Huh?"

"I'm at Dads. I called Pet. She will be expecting you within the hour to ride with her here."

"When did you get back in town?" I asked.

"Dude… What the fuck is *WRONG* with you? I told you this morning when I called that I'm on leave. Dad called me three days ago and told me Cora was on borrowed time."

"Oh. Jesus Christ, I seriously don't remember that conversation. When did she die?" I was slowly coming to the land of the living. Still thinking this conversation is not happening.

"An hour ago... around nine."

"Is Dad ok?"

"I don't know. It's too early to tell. Again, it's only been an hour."

I looked at the alarm clock. I forgotten the time in that short conversation. "Ok. Tell Pet I'm on my way."

"Ok. And we're staying the night. We have to go to the funeral home tomorrow to make arrangements and you're coming along."

"Sure, sure. Of course." I squeaked.

"Go to Pet's. I'll see you in a little while."

"Ok."

I broke connection. I was out of it. My world went fuzzy when Junior told me she was dead. My wish had come true. Jesus Christ I killed Cora. I wished her dead, she got cancer and it killed her.

I had no idea what day it was and now this news had piled on more disorientation. I threw on some clothes and ran out into the street forgetting my shoes. The warm pavement felt good on the soles of my feet. Shadows were cast everywhere by the buzzing streetlights. Pet's house was on the next street over and three blocks down. She was waiting for me in the front yard when I arrived and without a word we drove to Dad's house across town.

That night, we stayed with Dad to give him support. Cora was the second wife to have died on his watch so he was unstable at best, which was understandable. We wanted to keep an eye on him. We stayed up all night like we were little kids again having a sleepover. We told stories of better times back in the day. That's one thing we Benton siblings do. We sure like to talk about fond memories. I believe it gets us through the rough times like this, even though I didn't have any of Cora to share.

I squirted three tears at her wake. Dad asked if I was going to be alright, but my tears were the result of my emotions going through the wringer due to my drug use and general disorientation. I wasn't even there. My body was a shell. Mack showed up and told me before he walked in, he had stashed a bottle of brandy in the bushes out front. So we snuck out and walked to his house passing each other the bottle. We must have been quite a sight. I don't even like brandy, but it contained alcohol and it numbed the pain well.

Her funeral the next day was a lucid dream. Mack arrived at the house while I was getting ready and gave me some smoke as a gift of condolence. We stopped at his girlfriend's house on the way to the funeral in our suits and smoked the whole dime bag. It was exceptionally stronger than I was used to so I was completely obliterated. The funeral marched on like a zombie parade, foggy and lifeless. Amanda and Miriam showed up to support me. Amanda saw the state I was in and was insanely upset. I wouldn't see her again for two weeks. When I emerged looking to get laid, I had to eat crow for half the day until she finally calmed down. We ended up having one of our all night sex-a-thons at her grandparent's house while they vacationed in Florida that week. That did wonders for me.

Sonya and Junior had expressed their concern with Dad being left alone after the funeral. They proposed the idea of me going back home to help him out. I was *NOT* adamant about that idea. But they convinced me to *keep an eye on the old man.* So I agreed.

That first night back was weird for lack of a better word. All the memories of the dungeon came back to me but the restraint was gone. I no longer had an authority there in my old room. I spent years talked to the walls of what I would do if Cora was dead. I was so remorseful now because I had wished for it so many nights and now I got it. I was somehow responsible for her not being here anymore. The familiar guilt rushed back.

That night I had a dream Amanda and I were hastily stripping each other getting ready to have sex. We were in the passionate throws of ecstasy at her house and sloshing around on her waterbed. The walls were glowing a soft red like some sort of sex shop. I was caressing the soft curves of her body. After a long passionate kiss I pulled away from Amanda to find she had morphed into Cora. I awoke and realized I had been crying uncontrollably in my sleep. My face drenched with tears and a feeling of deep sorrow. I was back in the dungeon, and living my worst nightmare.

PART II
FREEDOM AND THE EXCESS

1

There is something about driving the winding roads through the mountains of Virginia and West Virginia in the late afternoon. The roads are lined with walls of rock showing layers of sediment that are millions of years old. I feel insignificant looking at beauty like this. Road trips have much to offer.

The cool wind of fresh mountain air blows through my hair. I remember the times I used to cruise in my truck at midnight with the windows down after an exceptionally hot summer day. I remember the warm air and Alice in Chains cranking out of my radio. Those were moments I would think of better times. Better times of friends before they moved on down the road of life. Those were therapeutic road trips.

I need some music. I could only take so much of the hum drum of traffic tires. I cruise the band and mostly find static. A few megahertz have country breaking through the static, or some evangelist talking about the brimstone of hell and how God was going to save you if you believe. Hallelujah.

"Come As You Are" by Nirvana breaks through on another station. That conjures feelings and memories of being in the dungeon back home. Songs like that helped me forget the pain and abuse. Memories of Cora's stereo glowing through the dark like a comforting beacon. I can still smell the years of dust that baked in the warmth of the flowing electricity in the receiver. The bass was so warm and inviting.

That's what songs are, right? They are little time machines that transport us to a moment that you cannot forget. I listen to the song as the signal gets stronger. Once the station is clear, it starts to fade again. By the time the song is over, I could barely hear it, and the moment is gone.

I turn off the radio. *It turned out to be such a nice afternoon.* The excitement of my new life to come is now straight ahead... And I can't wait for it any longer.

2

The next exit on my right advertises a Subway 0.2 miles nearby. *Perfect! I'm STARVING and I need fuel.* I pull into the Citgo station just off the interstate and start pumping. With my back against my truck, I stand motionless and listen to the country music that's piped into the speaker system while I wait for my truck to fill. *I'm thinking fifty bucks.*

The pump stops and I replace the lever, grab my receipt for fifty-six dollars, and head over to the Subway across the street. It stands alone from anything else on the corner. McDonalds and Burger King are on the other side of a parcel of land the size of a postage stamp and growing weeds the size of corn stalks.

I enter the shop and there are two teenage girls behind the counter. Blondie leans against the bread oven talking to a brunette wearing Ed Hardy under her apron. Ed Hardy clothing was cool... ten years ago.

"Welcome to Subway." Blondie says pawing the tiny bun of hair on top of her head.

"Howya doin," I say, "can I have a twelve inch chicken teriyaki on wheat, no cheese please."

"Toasted?" Blondie asks.

"No thanks."

The Brunette pipes in, "You ain't from 'round here huh?" I have a feeling I'm going to get this a lot when I settle in North Carolina.

"Nope, I'm from Buffalo." That's what I tell people because when I say I'm from Niagara Falls, they assume I'm Canadian.

"I can tell from your accent." The Brunette adds chewing her gum slack-jawed.

"It's that bad huh?"

"It's a thick'un. Whatcha want on the sammich?" Blondie asks.

"Spinach, extra tomatoes, very light onions please."

Blondie went to work while the Brunette stands and stares at me. I watch Blondie do her thing, all the while trying not to bust Ed Hardy's mistress. She is drilling holes through my face.

Blondie wraps up my sub. "So where ya goin?"

"North Carolina, starting a new job down there." I lie.

"That's fun. The Outer Banks is pretty. Oh well good luck."

"Thanks. Have a good day." I always do that. Three years in customer service right there.

"You too." Blondie says.

I walk to the door and turn back to the girls. The Brunette realizes she is caught staring. She turns to talk toward Blondie who is cleaning the counter and not paying any attention to her.

I walk across the tiny Subway parking lot, across the street, and back to the gas station where I left my truck at the gas pump. I drive over to the gas station store front, kill the engine and tear into my sandwich. I miss working out. It's been three days. In the passenger seat sits a box full of important keepsakes from my mother. It consists of a felt E.T. blanket she sown for me as well as a pair of baby overalls with "Beck's Transmission" and "Stephen" embroidered on the front pockets; various things like that. Cora had wrote, "Sandrea L. Benton, 1948-1983" on it in red marker. I stare at her handwriting as I ate my sandwich.

I think of the time Dad and Cora told me that my grandmother was not dead. *Boy, that fucks up an eight-year-olds head let me tell ya. That's four years of therapy all by itself.* My grandmother had schizophrenia so when she went off the reservation, Dad told me she died. She started taking her meds one day and decided to take Dad to court for visitation rights, and won. So Dad had to back pedal. We visited once, under the supervision of a social worker. She baked all these cookies for me that Cora promptly took away because she said they could be poisoned. She stuck them in the freezer. Junior and I used to steal them; they were just fine. Then she stopped taking her meds again and that was it. Dad told me she wanted to kidnap me after my mother died and my grandfather divorced her, so my grandfather had her committed. Dad did the best he could. I know that now. But that was a head job. I didn't know what to think.

I stuff the last bite of sub in my mouth and throw the wrapper in the passenger side floor board. I pull back on the road and see the Subway shop in my rearview mirror. *See ya ladies, there's a woman on the other side of this trip that you would never measure up too. No woman ever will.*

3

Sierra Ostergard was Amanda's best friend and she despised me like the plague. She was a tiny half-Italian, half-Swede beauty with curly black hair that flowed down her back like a dream. She had beautiful hazel eyes and skin tanned to the shade of mocha. Her body was perfect with a round compact behind you could bounce quarters on. But she was no use to me because she was a bigger prude than Miriam, if that was at all possible, and it was well known she didn't care for me anyway. She made a sport out of bad mouthing me to Amanda when I wasn't around. She had good reason to. I never treated Amanda that great. I wanted Amanda for one thing and Sierra knew it. Amanda was constantly fueling that fire to Sierra because she would tell her all the shenanigans I would get into.

A few weeks before school started back up, Amanda went to Disney World with her family. She had this brilliant idea to have Sierra hang out with me and keep me entertained while she was gone. I think she wanted her to keep tabs on me. I didn't mind. Regardless if Sierra liked me or not, she wore tight jean shorts, and I would be more than happy to stare at that beautiful ass for a few days.

Surprisingly, she was nice to me. We hung out for the week talking, going to lunch, or watching movies. Her favorite pastime was shopping, and one afternoon we went to The Gap. I was trying on a shirt she wanted me to buy and when I stuck my head through the changing area curtain to ask her opinion, she was standing in front of it and her face was right in front of mine. I leaned in and pecked her on the lips. Who knows why I did that. It was a good idea at the time. We walked back to her house in silence about ten blocks from the shopping mall.

Her house was a nice two story, with light green siding and a bridge over the creek in the back yard. On the front porch a white wooden swing was anchored to the ceiling in front of a huge bay window. From the outside, the house looked neat and maintained.

Inside the house was as neat as the outside. An overflowing magazine rack by the recliner in the far corner was the only mess in the living room. The pillows on the couch matched the recliner which was a cool shade of gray. An oak coffee table sprawled on a tan throw rug in the middle of the floor that looked comfortable enough to sleep on. We set our bags on the couch on our way to the kitchen. There was an island with pots and pans hanging from the ceiling. Sierra hopped up and sat on the counter which was granite. She looked so hot that day. She wore this white halter with lace trim. I could see her nipples under the material. As we talked I kept inching over to her. Finally I leaned in and we started making out. Her tight little frame was warm, soft, and comfortable. She pressed her tiny breasts against me as we kissed. She wrapped her legs around my waist and my hands fell to her hips like they belonged there. I wanted her so bad I couldn't hardly stand it.

Her father came through the back door and damn near caught us. I scampered away to the other side of the kitchen. He nods at Sierra, fumbles for something on the counter next to her, and disappears into the living room. We giggled like elementary kids. This was very confusing to me. I thought Sierra hated me with a passion for treating Amanda the way I did. These were insanely mixed signals.

When I left her, I fantasized about her the entire walk

home. I wanted to see her naked so bad. She was gorgeous; perfectly molded by an artist, and it made me sad. I knew she would never give me the time of day despite what just happened. I just wasn't her type. So I pushed her out of my head and had forgotten the incident with her by the time I met up with Mack for a night of debauchery.

4

By the time I awoke from my drug induced haze in September, I realized I flunked three required classes my junior year and had to repeat them to graduate in the summer. I was already behind the eight-ball. Senior year started slam packed with work and a week in I was drowning with homework and studying. Girls were on my mind, not my studies and I was losing interest at an alarming rate.

There was this smoking hot blonde that worked the register at the mini-mart just up the road from my house. Her hair fell in perfect ringlets that barely touched her shoulders and her curvy hips were just like I like them. She stood eye to eye with me, had sun kissed skin, and a small wire ring pierced in the left side of her nose. Unbeknownst to me she expressed an interest.

One night I walked into the mini-mart about fifteen minutes before it closed and asked for a pack of cigarettes. She convinced me to keep her company while she closed the store. I was planning to go home; given it was a school night. But I was a sucker for a beautiful woman, especially a woman that dripped sexual prowess and looked like she stepped out of a harlequin romance novel. She resembled Joan Osborne, *What if God was one of uuuuusss....* The next night we ended up at her place and you know the rest.

We started hanging out. She wanted to keep the relationship a secret because she was twenty-two and I was seventeen and still considered a minor in New York State. The secret was safe with me for two reasons. One, she was gorgeous and I wanted to keep fucking her as long as possible. And two, there was this little problem with me having a girlfriend.

A few weeks later, on an ordinary Saturday, I planned on meeting up with Mack around ten at his house. I was trying to set myself straight in school to no avail and saving the partying for the weekends. After spending a Friday night with Mack gallivanting around town, he called around three on this particular Saturday afternoon and told me he made plans to go to a girl's house he knew to *get down* as he put it. We set up a rendezvous for us to smoke and maybe hang out afterwards. At five o'clock I had time to kill so I called a mutual friend of ours.

Kristie LaGuardia is a small round half-Italian, half-African with full lips, and a baby-faced flawless complexion. I met Kristie through Mack and had only known her for a few months. She suggested I hang out and watch a movie with her. Her house was the place where random kids were constantly coming and going. It was a happening place because her parents weren't home half the time.

When I arrived two guys I knew from school were there. I didn't know them well, but I knew they were stoners like me. One of them, Tommy, sat on the ratty couch by the front door on the phone with a cigarette hanging from his fingers. He put the cigarette to his lips and the two inch ash broke off and fell onto his lap. He brushed the ashes to the floor and with the phone receiver still in his ear he piped up and said he was going to score some weed and asked if I wanted to get in with him. *I never say no to hippie spinach.* So around eight o'clock, Tommy and the other guy, I didn't know his real name but everyone called him Gringo due to his Mexican heritage, got a call and the three of us were off to score our dope.

It was an ordinary transaction. They rode their bikes and I jogged to the end of the street. Then we hung a right to the next block over. We met up with the dealer, scored, rolled up a fat joint—what they called a dooberonic—right there on the corner and we passed it around. It was nothing special. Tommy's sister met us there to pinch a little for herself. I started rolling around in the street and giggling my fool head off.

"What the fuck is wrong with this guy?!?" Tommy's sister asked.

"I don't know, maybe he's a rookie." Gringo said.

"Sorry guys," I said as I got up still giggling, "That never happens."

"Well, it is good stuff, I only get the best." Tommy added.

"Yeah man. I feel ya." I said. *I've had better.*

"You got a hold of yourself?" Tommy asked.

I barely held back my giggles. "Yeah, I do now."

"Let's go back to Kristie's." Gringo added. "We're asking for the fuzz hangin out in the open like this."

We started walking back to Kristie's house. The last thing we wanted was some nosy doughnut muncher to drive by and get curious. As I turned the corner back on her street something changed.

"We're gonna sleep like champs tonight." Gringo

said.

"No doubt." I answered.

Right then a feeling of euphoria completely washed my body. Tommy and Gringo rode nonchalantly down the street.

"WOW!" I exclaimed. "I feel like a little kid again!"

Tommy and Gringo found that hilarious. I looked down the street and everything was crystal clear. It was the most beautiful feeling I had ever felt. Then, I felt like I had been there before. Everything I was doing at that exact point I had done a million times before. I felt I knew what was going to happen next. It was the strangest feeling I had ever felt in my life, and it was starting to scare me. Tommy and Gringo dumped their bikes in Kristie's front yard and ran up the porch steps. I followed them in the house. They flopped on Kristie's couch, and I walked past the coffee table to look for Kristie in the kitchen and BAM....

I blacked out.

When I came too, I was sprawled out on my back in the living room and Tommy and Gringo's faces were looking over me.

"Look," Gringo said, "his head's busted open." Then they were gone. I was in a fog. The Kristie's little sister's face appeared.

"Yeah, he's bleeding." She said. "I'm calling 9-1-1."

A few minutes later, that registered and I snapped awake. *Shit! They're calling the fuzz and I'm stoned out of my mind. This is not going to end good.* I arose from the floor and walked out to the front porch. Kristie's sister was standing in the yard. Tommy and Gringo had boogalooed when they found out the heat was coming. I would never see them again. I sat down on the steps and the shadows of the night started playing tricks on me.

"Are you ok?" Kristie's sister asked. I didn't reply. I was shaking so she got the blanket off the couch and put it around my shoulders. Seconds felt like hours. The weird feelings came back worse that before the blackout. I felt like everything was scripted. I thought I knew exactly what she was going to do and say next, down to every last detail. I had an overwhelming feeling of déjà vu. I felt I was locked in a never ending loop of events. It was like everything in the universe revolved in a circle and at that moment, I was experiencing that exact moment in time again for the millionth time. The sensation scared the living shit out of me. I got up and started walking home. Home was three blocks away.

"But wait!" Kristie's sister yelled after me. "Help is coming for you."

"I have to go home." I said. "I have to see if I still live there." I thought that this wasn't happening. This was a dream or I had passed through another dimension or a time warp. So I was heading home to see if my dad and I were in fact living there. I was confused beyond belief. I walked home, wave upon wave of emotions were hitting me. It was almost like I was looking through panels of different dimensions. This was beyond weird and terrifying. I saw everything crystal clear, then insane déjà vu, then mass confusion. Everything in the universe revolved in a circle. Everything was stuck on repeat.

Half way to my house, a patrol car careened by the road and a cop hopped out. The cars strobe lights started a new wave of déjà vu and tears started streaming from my eyes. The officer tried to restrain me so I punched him in the face. He tackled me to the ground, hog-tied and handcuffed me with thick zip ties before I even knew any better. I continued to struggle and battle for what seemed like forever. He knelt on my neck and I couldn't breathe. Another cop had arrived within the melee at the scene and sat on my chest. I was choking for life.

The authorities called my dad and caught him just after he had gone to bed. He drove to the hospital showing up in wrinkled clothes and flip flops, hair all disheveled, and found me handcuffed to the gurney charged with assault on a police officer. It was quite a predicament I got myself into. I was looking at some jail time; probably in juvie. Dad wanted answers so I gave vague details of what happened because my brain was scrambled, then I passed out again.

When I awoke again a nurse appeared over me and shoved a bottle in my face and said if I didn't piss in it, they would have to shoot a catheter up my dick. So I peed in the jar. It was then I realized the cuffs were gone. I thought I had dreamed them.

The ride home was silent. I was destroyed. I just wanted to crawl in bed and stay there for a month. When I got home I trudged up the stairs to my familiar steaming hot dungeon and flopped in bed. About three-thirty the afternoon, Dad poked his head in my bedroom doorway.

"Shorty, you wanna watch the Broncos? They're the four o'clock game."

"Sure." I said. *Jesus,* I thought. *I must have slept all day.* I got out of bed and threw on my ripe soccer shorts that were piled in the corner. I went to the bathroom, took a long four minute piss, flushed the toilet, and looked at myself in the mirror.

Fuck! I didn't dream this. I thought. There was a small bandage over my right eyebrow covering four or five stitches. *I didn't dream that. I did get fucked up and smash my head on Kristie's coffee table. That means when I go down stairs, Dad is going to kill me and bury me in the garden out back, awesome.*

I strolled downstairs through the dining room and sat on the couch. The Denver Broncos were in Irving, Texas to play the Dallas Cowboys. All through my life I grew up with football in my blood. Cora would only let me watch a half hour of the Bills game or the Broncos if they were on. Now she was gone, it felt weird to sit and watch football with my dad for a few hours.

"How'd the Bills do?" I asked.

"Carolina never got off the bus." Dad had a notebook he kept scores in because he had three or four parlay tickets going on any given Sunday. The Bills trounced the Panthers 31-9. He had one winner so far. Someone knocked at the front door. Dad got up and answered it letting Kristie and her older sister in.

"How you feeling?" Kristie asked.

"Foggy."

"He's a little worse for wear. But he'll be alright." Dad said. "He'll be back on his feet in no time."

Kirstie's sister waddled by the wall. Her girth blocked the light coming through the front door. "I want to assure you that drug use at our house isn't tolerated, Mr. Benton. This was a freak incident. Shorty will be banned from our house if it happens again."

"I appreciate hearin that, but I think he learned his lesson."

"He better've." She shot me a serious look. She was a bitchy woman anyway.

"I got this for you." Kristie handed me a Boston CD; their debut album from 1976. "I remember you talking about it a few weeks ago."

"Thanks. You're sweet." She sat on the couch and gave me a hug. She smelled like coco butter. "I'll be back on my feet in no time."

"Ok."

They exchanged pleasantries with Dad and left. Dad and I sat in silence. My throat was throbbing in pain. I thought it was going to explode out of my neck at any moment.

"You're covered on my insurance until you're nineteen. So the medical bills will be taken care of. How much money ya have in your bank account?"

"Last I checked, about 450 dollars." I answered.

"Well, you're gonna to give that to me. The 600 dollar ambulance ride isn't covered. We'll call it even. I'll pay for stupidity once, but that's it. After that you are on your own."

"Ok." I was beaten. Nothing I could say.

That was the extent of our talk about that situation. I had gotten off easy. But when Dad said after one freebie you're on your own, he meant it.

We continued to watch the game. If I recall correctly, Elway got injured in the third quarter and never returned. They weren't doing much anyway. The 31-21 score was closer that the game really was. My Broncos never had a chance.

5

A few weeks later I met up with Mini-mart girl again. "Wow. That night was crazy, huh?" She asked.

"You have no idea." I said, lighting a cigarette from the free pack of Camel Filters she gave me. "How'd you find out?"

"I was working, just had to look out the window." The store was a stone's throw away from where the cop tackled me like I was a quarterback scrambling for his life from a gorilla linebacker. I explained to her the feelings I felt that night.

"I bet you were having an anxiety attack. One time, I was at a Bison's game with a friend of mine, and I like, looked over at her and she was curled up in the fetal position almost under her seat. She said it was an anxiety attack." She pulled a drag from her Marlboro light.

"Well, whatever it was it sucks."

"So you ok?"

"Yeah, my dad knew the cop. He was going to press charges, assault on a police officer, but as a favor to my dad, he didn't file it."

She softly bounced a leg in place as she stood in front of me. She was turned on by my new bad boy status. "You're making me so fucking horny right now."

Her candidness shocked me. We started making out in the back room of the store. I remember tasting the cigarette on her tongue and it was turning me on something crazy. She would periodically go calmly to the register whenever customers came in, and then return to me in the back room. After she closed the store, we drove around the corner and found a dark place to park down a dead end road to handle our business. She used me like I was using Amanda.

A few weeks later, I was at Mini-mart girl's house smoking a joint and the crazy feelings of confusion and fear happened all over again. I told her to take me home. She dropped me off at my house just when the déjà vu stopped. I figured I should just call her back but I decided to stay home. It was a good thing I did. I went upstairs and turned on Cora's stereo very low like I liked to do when I'm trying to go to sleep. All night I had waves of déjà vu. I saw the exact same thing at Kristie's that other night. But how could I? *It doesn't make sense. I just did it.* I thought. *I can't see the future. This does not make sense!!!* This was scaring the shit out of me.

Earlier that night Mini-mart girl and I went to her other job where she worked at the VFW where she tended bar. That was running through my head like I was in two places at once. I laid in my bed and faded away to the bar and back to my bed. I thought if I stayed in bed, I'll be ok. *Just stay in bed.*

The next morning I vowed never to smoke weed again. *This déjà vu shit is for the BIRDS,* I thought. Mini-mart girl started banging some other guy and told me we shouldn't hang out any more. That was the end of Mini-mart girl. That hurt because she taught me so much, and I was having a GREAT time.

Now I knew what Amanda felt when I treated her this way.

6

After that, Mack and I started a bad routine; one of many. Three or four nights a week we would get together, he would smoke weed, *burn trees,* he would say, and I would get shitfaced because there was no way in hell I was gonna smoke. He teased me constantly about it too. Because of this new routine, I would sleep in to nine or ten in the morning because Dad was up and out the door to work by quarter to seven by the time I had to regularly get up for school. I would miss the first two sometimes three classes. When I finally woke up from that bender, I found that not only was I going to fail the three classes I was repeating from my junior year, I was also going to fail my whole senior year and have to repeat next year and attend summer school after that. I wasn't having it, so I dropped out. Mack dropped out in his sophomore year so it wasn't a shock to him.

In March of my senior year, while everyone was making plans for prom and graduation, I was in the main office at school with Sonya withdrawing from class. Dad was disappointed but never showed it. He had a point. I was an honor student up until the second semester of junior year. Girls and partying had won out; a battle I regret that I lost.

Mack had started to break into people's houses and steal things to get money. Stupid if you ask me, so I wasn't surprised when he got pinched. Denny cut a deal with the Judge sentencing the case whom he knew from his cop connections. The deal was, no jail time if he left town and lived with family for a while.

Mack was sent to live with his Uncle in Syracuse. I visited him once. Syracuse is a cool college town with various streets with little shops and restaurants. We traipsed along the streets acting like we were gangsters until Mack told me he missed being back home because he had no friends in Syracuse. I knew how he felt. I lost my partner in crime for a while and it sucked big time.

I started to hang out with Barney Lombardo again after I ran into him at a party. He was still hanging out with Amanda, Miriam, and Sierra on the regular. I still wanted to be around them. Especially Miriam who I had realized I was completely in love with. He also had a job, his own apartment and a fridge full of beer whenever I showed up to hang out.

Amanda and I had great sex. She booked a room for my eighteenth birthday at the Econo Lodge on Niagara Falls Boulevard because, of course, she was so in love with me and I was oblivious. Barney and the gang came over and we swam in the heated pool. Barney and Sierra we splashing and playing around by themselves in the deep end. They were in a fresh relationship and they acted like it. Amanda, Miriam and I were standing in the shallow end generally talking about nothing. I remember looking at Miriam in her bikini and wanting her instead of Amanda to hang out with that night and feeling so jealous of the guy she was talking about. I wanted to untie the strings on her bathing suit in the worst way.

After everyone left and Amanda and I were left to our vises. The room had mirrors on the wall, and a California king sized bed with a small two person Jacuzzi in the bathroom. The bathroom had a half wall so you could watch a movie from the Jacuzzi. We had great fun that night.

I got a call a month later.

"We need to talk." *Shit*. I thought. *This isn't good*. I

knew right away. It was six weeks after my birthday. Amanda's voice echoed in my head. *No, don't pullout. It feels so good!!*

"What's going on?"

"I'm pregnant." She said. I knew before she even said it.

"What are we going to do?" *I can handle this. I'm not running away.*

"We can take care of this."

"If that's what you wanna do? I support you in any way."

"My mom doesn't want you to be a part of this. She said either we get an abortion which she will pay for, or we have the baby and my grandparents will help raise it, and the baby will have their last name."

I knew where this was going. She wanted to cut me out of the equation. "Do what you think is right." I said. "I support anything you want to do."

"Ok. We've made an appointment with the Doctor to have an abortion. My mom also said when this was all said and done, you should stay away from me."

"Whatever your mom wants." I said, knowing Amanda couldn't stay away from me, and I was right.

7

Dad said since I dropped out I couldn't live with him anymore. "When I was seventeen I was already in the Army." *Pull up your socks and earn your keep.*

"It's a different time now. There is no way I can afford an apartment!" I pleaded.

"HUSTLE! Wake up, get two jobs, whatever it takes. You can handle it. I raised you to be tough. Only Shorty can take care of Shorty. I'm not gonna."

"I'm trying! I'm getting my GED because no one will hire an eighteen year old drop out."

"I was in South America when I was eighteen. You've done nothin. What a shame." He shook his head at me. I'm already the black sheep and his great disappointment. "Your mother would have kicked you in the ass. She wouldn't have let you drop out."

I could not believe I was having this conversation with him. I was eighteen and broke. *How the fuck am I supposed to survive?*

"I'm looking Dad! I swear to God."

"You have one more month. After that you're on the street. Wake up and smell the tulips." *Harsh.*

As fate would have it, two weeks later I scored a job at Builder's Square. Sonya figured I needed help so we split the rent on a two bedroom apartment located on Seventieth Street just off the main Boulevard, just a short five block walk from work. It was perfect.

While the Class of '96 was living it up that June at Prom and graduation, I was blowing lines for the first time with my sister.

Sonya had a boyfriend named Abe who was only three years older than I was. He was a good six-three, about 240 pounds and never wore a shirt. He could buy beer legally and had a sweet drug hook up. There was a pay phone in the parking lot at the Wilson Farms just down the road. He would drive up, throw a quarter into the slot, call his dealer and let the phone ring twice, then hang up. The dealer on the other end knew it was Abe by the pay phone number showing up on his caller ID. He knew where to find him and make the drop.

It was a great system. We would go back to the apartment, chop up lines on a Metallica mirror I won at Six Flags some years back, and go off bar hopping all night because you do not get drunk when you're also bumping lines. As a bonus, I wasn't having those déjà vu episodes when I was on blow either. It was my new favorite drug.

One night I went with Abe and a few of his friends to score an eight-ball at the drop off. After a few minutes a guy shows up by the driver side window, whistling, noticed Abe's chest pocket on his shirt was slightly hanging open, chucked the eight-ball perfectly in pocket, turned around and walked away dancing down the street. He was so zooted, he never asked for the money. A few hours later when that was gone, we got another from him, two for one that night.

Another time we were hanging out playing euchre and we heard a knock at the door. Before Abe answered the door, he strategically placed his pack of smokes on top of the pile of devils dandruff that was on the kitchen table where we were playing. The cigarettes barely covered it all. He answers the door and it was the police. I was shitting bricks. They walked around the place and politely told us to quiet down. Sonya, knowing pretty much everyone in the city, knew one of the officers and was talking a mile a minute at him. I noticed Abe's nose running pink snot and sweating bullets. His chest was gleaming with perspiration. They would have easily brought us all to jail if one of them accidently bumped into the kitchen table.

One night, I did so much blow with Abe, I drank way

too much and gave myself alcohol poisoning. I passed out on the bathroom floor, which was grimy with dirt and piss stains by the rim of the toilet. Abe and Sonya dragged my dead weight to my room where I slept on a futon bed. Periodically she checked on me through the night. She saved my life by keeping me on my side so I would not drown in my own vomit. I came to a day later and immediately got drunk again not learning a thing from my stupidity. I didn't even thank her after she told me I shivered all night despite feeling warm and sweaty. Those were dark times of personal struggle for me. I was trying to find my way and failing miserably.

Mack came back to the city after six months in Syracuse. The night he came back, he smoked a fat joint with Abe, ran out of the apartment and projectile spewed in the hallway. His body couldn't take the weed after being sober for six months. He should have stayed in Syracuse. I was totally on self-destruct and I had my partner in crime back. It was only natural that I dragged him back into the life and we were a dangerous combination together. We disappeared for days on end with various girls or seedy characters. I drained my account frequently on cocaine through my connection with Abe. Sonya was at her wits end with me so she did not renew the apartment lease when it lapsed and moved into a house across town with Abe. I reluctantly moved back home with Dad to endure his holier than thou shit storm of dime story psychology.

8

The best thing I did after I dropped out—in between all the drugs and benders—was acquire my GED. I signed up downtown at the Educational Community Center and showed up one Saturday in November and aced the test. This is a place where all the fuck ups go when they are kicked out of public school. All the blow I snorted hadn't destroyed my brain at all. The test was so basic a monkey could have passed it. When I came home this last time, Dad hounded me about what I was going to do with my life, since I lost my last job a few months prior and had been unemployed since.

"I got my GED!"

"Great. Ya goin to college yet?"

"I was thinking about it." It was on my radar.

"Well since you're not going, I have some savings bonds I need you to sign."

"I have savings bonds?" I asked.

"Yeah, I bought them for you kids. But I need help with the last of Cora's medical bills."

"Ok."

"You have about twelve hundred dollars. Since you're not goin to college, I'll give you ten percent. I need them for medical bills."

"That can come in handy for college Dad. I need that."

"You didn't even know it existed until I told ya."

"What if I don't sign them?"

"I can get them signed. It will just take longer without your signatures. You want the hundred and twenty dollars or what?"

"Whatever. Take the money, I don't care anyway. If it's that important to you, take it."

"I am, and it is important. Thank you."

Robbed by my own father, *what a dick*! It wouldn't be the last time I would find he took money from me either.

My dad was shifty like that. He knew a hundred ways to skim off the top. I guess it comes from growing up poor in the forties and fifties. That little stunt pissed me off to no end. But of course, I never told him. I was afraid to tell him how I felt. I guess it was residual from being raised the way I was.

Mack got worse with his drug habits. He started dabbling with ecstasy and going to raves in Buffalo. He would tell me stories of the stuff he did at those raves. They sounded like big sweaty orgies with dish suds. Sounded fantastic but I wasn't going to fry my brain on that stuff. He was also going down the road to petty crime to pay for his various habits so I hung out with him less. It hurt me because we were best friends. *Guilty by Association they call it Shorty.* Dad would tell me. *If he robs a bank, you go to jail with him, Guilty by Association.* So I started "missing his calls" until he just stopped coming around.

Dad decided to rent the upstairs apartment. He decided to install a cooling system up there for the new tenants. That sure would have come in handy when I was stuck in the dungeon. Being so close to the roof, the upstairs would bake to eighty-five, sometimes ninety degrees. At night I would ask if I could sleep down stairs in the air conditioning but Cora would tell me to *get my stupid ass back upstairs before she let me have it.* I remember the air feeling so good on my warm skin and trudging back upstairs through a wall of heat almost in tears.

This was a fine idea because the upstairs still haunted me. Ghosts still roamed while I thought of Cora and how different my life would be if my mother was still alive. The walls still told stories of the scared little boy that used to dwell there. A confused boy who wished his stepmother dead while lying in his bed at night with his hand in his pants.

9

I moved my things in the room at the front of the house just off center from the front porch, and it was easy access for nightly visitors. Dad started dating a lady that a friend had introduced him to and was spending the night at her house frequently. I would be alone in this big house by myself with the demons and monsters that lurked upstairs.

Some friends I knew through Kristie LaGuardia would stop by all hours of the night and ease that pain. I would be lying in bed about ten or eleven at night and be awoken by a sweet voice outside my window. They would climb through and we'd have sex all over the house. It was the late nineties. The era of "Slick Willy" Clinton. I was a charmer and getting laid was easy.

One night I heard Miriam's voice outside my window. She never wanted to have sex of course, but I wished she would just once.

She had turned into a stunner after she had graduated and spent some time in the summer sun. Her blonde hair had grown to the middle of her back, and had lost a few pounds. She was a little compact beauty now with mesmerizing hips. She knew she drove me crazy. We would hang out at her house where she had a hot tub on her back deck. She would wear these little bikinis that barely covered her. She especially liked a green polka dot two piece that tied at both hips and on her shoulders. I so wished it accidently untied and fell off so I could see what she had. Being the major prude she was, she had this habit of making out with me and then stopping when it got too intense. On more than one occasion, I have begged her to have sex or just let me perform oral with no return favor, but she would leave me with a raging hard on because she could. I told her that I loved her, and I had loved her since I met her, which was true. She was beautiful and I would kill the world for her.

So it went on like that for a while. I told her she could call me at any time, day or night, and when she did, I ran over to her house as fast as I could. We would hang out, watch movies, listen to the latest music, or just lounge around and talk; which half the time led to me pleading with Miriam desperately to let me eat her.

She decided to go to Community College in the fall. She thought if she took a year off, she would never go. I had taken a year off, but decided to enroll as well. I wanted to stay as close to her as possible. My thinking was if I stayed close to her, she would realize I was her knight in shining armor. I was so naïve. I chose the Fine Arts program due to my love of drawing, and my long college career begun. Amanda and Sierra also enrolled. Sierra had just broken up with Barney after about a year of courtship. She had lost about fifteen pounds and looked a little shaken from the experience but she was dealing. The old gang was together again.

"Sierra ok?" I asked. We were waiting for her in the main lobby. It was a vast open place, much bigger than most Community Colleges. "She looks like she lost weight."

"She's a little faded right now from the Barney debacle." Amanda said.

"He was a jerk." Miriam piped in. "He disappeared a

lot. And he stole from her."

I haven't seen Barney in a few months. But we were still buddies. So it was a little harsh for me to hear these horror stories about him. They did sound familiar though. Like the stuff I used to do to Amanda. *Was I really that much of a dickhead?*

"How is your relationship going with Brett, Amanda?" Miriam asked. Amanda had a new squeeze which I had heard through the grapevine. He was my carbon copy.

"Awesome! That guy is so in love with me, he doesn't know what to do with himself."

Hardly, I thought. *She's laying it on think.*

"Barney and Sierra finally had sex. She's not a virgin anymore. Did I tell you that?" Amanda asked. There was a gleam in her eye you could have seen from space, and she directed it right at me. Like she wanted to hurt me with this news.

"What do I care about the sex life of your prude friends?" I said to her. I hid it well. It did sting. I didn't know why.

Sierra strolled up wearing a leather jacket and her class book under her arm. Her hair was frizzy and crawling down her back. She looked like a greaser's girl from "The Outsiders."

"Look at this one," she pointed at me, "he has books in his hand. He's a walking oxymoron."

"Touché lady, touché." I nodded.

Amanda and Sierra split off toward their class. "You want to grab some breakfast?" Miriam asked me. "They have really good breakfast sandwiches."

"Yeah, that sounds good."

We walked down the hall toward the cafeteria, which was a hop, skip, and a jump from us. The Culinary Curriculum was the best in the state and the student loved to work the kitchens. We were the only two there that morning. We ordered egg and cheese on English muffins that had this delightful hollandaise drizzle on them.

"It's a shame you and Amanda never worked out. You guys were good together." She said chewing a bite of her muffin.

"Not anymore. I love you. That ruins things for other ladies." I winked at her and wiped a crumb from the corner of her mouth with my napkin.

"I know you do." She said softly.

"Besides." I added. "After our abortion it wasn't the same for us."

Miriam stared at me wild eyed. Her jaw hit the floor. "You got her pregnant?!?"

I shrugged. "Yeah. I though you knew."

"NO. This is news to me!! She had two?!?"

"No, no, no." I shook my finger at her. "She only had one, with me. She lied to Colin to get back at him." Colin was Amanda's boyfriend before me; some jock strap. Amanda had the brilliant idea to tell everyone at school she had aborted Colin's child to get back at him because he had cheated on her. I never said she was bright. "Only one. She's not using abortions for birth control. She had one mistake. With me. She's not some whore."

"I was gonna say, that was a bit much." A section of hair was hanging in her left eye. She tucked it behind her ear.

"I know." I said in agreement. "It was a fucked up time."

"Well, class is about to start." She had a few bites of her sandwich left. "You want the rest of this?"

I had wolfed mine down. I was eyeballing hers anyway. I took it from her plate. "Yeah, thanks. I'll call you later ok?"

"Sure." She got up and turned to walk out. I watched her hips sway from side to side and again felt sad that she didn't love me the way I loved her. It was ripping me up inside.

A few hours later I was outside the rec room reading over my calculus class notes. They might as well been in Mandarin Chinese. Out the corner of my eye, I saw Amanda walking up the hall. "Hey baby. What's shakin'?" I said to her still looking at my notes.

"Don't 'hey baby' me you little shit!"

I looked up. She had steam coming out of her ears. "What? What's wrong?!?"

"You told Miriam about our abortion. You were supposed to keep it a secret!"

"I was clearing it up to save your reputation. She thought you had two so I was setting it straight. She knew about the one. I was saving your reputation that's all." I pleaded.

"My reputation doesn't need saving. I never want to talk to you again!" And she stormed away down the hall. I sat in shock.

A kid in the rec room said, "Wow!"

"She's pissed." Said another. I picked up my books and scampered down the hall to catch up with Amanda. I got to the door at the end that led to the courtyard and burst through it. I looked around in the cool fall afternoon sun, but she was long gone.

That afternoon at Miriam's house we talked about the situation. She had heard the entire run down from Sierra. Amanda was excitable. She reveled in situations like this. If she was the center of it, even better.

"She doesn't want to talk to me anymore. She's pretty upset. I was trying to help her situation. I don't want you to believe she was having all these abortions, you know?" I shuffled my feet on the living room carpet. It was blue shag.

"I know. She's upset with me too. But she will come around. She always does."

"I hope you're right. She seems pretty upset. She won't return my calls."

"That could be Brett's doing."

"Wow! That makes a lot of sense now."

"Yeah, he's so far up her ass, it's sickening."

"Like me with you?" I shrugged.

She smacked me on the shoulder. "No, you're different." She said as she turned her gaze to the ground. She had me wrapped around her finger. I was hopeless.

"Let's get together again." I launched into it, threw caution to the wind one last time. "Start at square one, like we just met."

Miriam looked into my eyes and flashed a smile full of pity. Her little sister walked through the front door. The resemblance was uncanny except for her dark straight hair. "Johnnie is waiting for you out front Miriam." She flopped on the couch next to me. "Hey Shorty, how's it goin?"

"Hey Taylor, what's up?"

"I gotta go, Johnnie is waiting." Miriam opened the door to the front porch and looked back at me. Her eyes oozed sympathy. "See you later Shorty."

She exited. I had to follow her. I got up from the couch and ran out to the porch. Taylor followed. "Wait!!" I yelled to Miriam.

Rain was pissing down in ropes. A mustang emitted muffled thumps by the front curb. I jumped down all four porch steps in a single bound. The rain was immediately saturating. Miriam and I stood in her front yard looking like two wet abandoned dogs. The water was making her clothes stick and it revealed her layers.

"I can't do this anymore!" I shouted. "I want to be your friend. I am your friend...."

"I know." Miriam said.

"Don't get in the car with him." I pointed to the thumping mustang that was wiping waves of water from its windshield at us. "I can make you happy. Let me try again."

"I gotta go." She grabbed the door handle.

"Please Miriam," she looked back at me with her hand still on the car; hair matted and dripping, "I love you. And I always will."

She opened the door. A filthy sample of garbage music spilled out in the air. "I know." She shouted over the noise.

She got in the mustang and Johnnie the fucktard put an arm around her shoulder. She looked at me and pressed her hand to the window. I waved back and Johnnie the fucktard screams the mustang down the street and out of sight.

I looked back to the porch and Taylor was standing with her arms crossed by the front door. I ran back up the stairs.

"I don't understand. She said she likes me but she won't date me. She is so confusing." I said to Miriam's sister. I was dripping into a growing puddle next to her.

"You know her by now." Taylor said. "She's all about the chase. She chased you and got you. Now she's not interested. She will just hurt you in the end anyway, you know this."

"Yeah." I agreed, feeling rain drip from my chin.

"Just move on, you deserve better than her anyway."

Deep down I felt she was right. But I was gluten for punishment. That night I went home soggy and defeated. That was the last I saw of Miriam for more than a decade.

10

By the time my beloved Broncos beat the Packers in the Super Bowl, I started a new job testing oxygen valves at a place called Westwood Valve working the midnight shift. It was an old dusty open warehouse with water tanks scattered along the property like fence posts. Now that Amanda hated me, Miriam and Sierra dropped off the face of the planet, and Mack was off doing who knows what drug with whom, I immersed myself with work. I had "postponed" my college career because I had no means of transportation to get to class. My routine every day consisted of rolling out of bed around nine or ten, eat what Dad had set aside for my dinner, work from eleven to seven in the morning, after work cook scrambled eggs and spam, watch "Gargoyles" cartoon reruns on USA network from eight to nine, then go to bed. I would sleep the day away because midnights screw with your balance. On the weekends I couldn't sleep so I stayed up watching "Twilight Zone" and "Tales from the Crypt" reruns into the wee hours of the night on HBO. It's quiet and creepy in the stillness with the flickering light from the television. I felt lost and alone.

One night at Westwood a group of new temps were shown around the place and one of them was girl I knew named Joey LaBeouf. In sixth grade, we went on a field trip to an ice skating rink. I couldn't skate for shit. Every five minutes or so I would get a good rhythm going until this cute little girl would come flying by and crash into me sending me sprawling to the floor. She thought it was hilarious. Some years later, that same little girl got a job working the front registers at McDonalds. We had a laugh reminiscing about that time she was knocking me around the skating rink.

She had had a little boy since I had worked with her at McAmerica, and was currently going through a divorce after a six month marriage. She was still smoking hot. Curves in all the right places, blond hair down her back that bounced when she walked, and a compact behind in her jeans I could not take my eyes off of. We hit it off immediately. We thought it was fate that we kept running into each other. I showered her with gifts. I bought her all sorts of jewelry, and we had amazing sex. She had told me she never loved anyone like she loved me. After six months we were engaged. We were nineteen, and so dumb. But the relationship soured immediately after I asked. She started having male roommates and I knew she was fucking them. One night I babysat her son while she went out with "a friend." Later I found out she fucked him too.

One night she needed a ride to work. She had quit Westwood and got a job at Walmart. I dropped her off and left her and the relationship at the curb that night.

I was crushed. I immediately realized the reason I loved Joey so much. She was a carbon copy of Miriam with one difference; Joey gave it up to me. I realized it was always about Miriam. I walked the streets at night thinking about her. I would look up at the Orion Constellation, which was Miriam's favorite, and would wonder what she was doing at that moment, wondering if we were doing the exact same thing. Again, naïve.

When I couldn't sleep at night I would walk by Miriam's house. She probably wasn't ever home but that didn't deter me from walking by. It was the physical place I could visit and remember her, and wish to see her again.

One afternoon I walked down her street and to my dismay, a family was moving into her house. I was beyond crushed. She was completely gone somewhere, not giving one single solitary thought to my whereabouts. At that moment I decided to grow up. Well, mostly.

11

I slipped back into my routine of working midnights, spam and eggs, and "Gargoyles" reruns. One night before work I worked up the courage to make a phone call.

"Hello?" The voice answered. It was the voice of a lady that spent years smoking and living the life of a barfly.

"Is Amanda there?"

"Hold on." The raspy voice said. I was grateful she didn't ask who I was. She would have hung up on me. In the background I heard Amanda say, "Thanks, Mom."

"Hello?"

"It's me." I said. She knew immediately.

"What do you want?" She asked. Her tone was sour, annoyed at the voice in her ear.

"Just five minutes of your time and I'll be out of your hair, can you do that? I have to talk to you. Can I meet you somewhere?"

"Not tonight I have plans."

"Tomorrow then? I need to do this. I'll meet you somewhere."

"I'll come to you. Where will you be?"

"Dad's."

"I'll be there at eight o'clock. You have five minutes." Then she abruptly hung up.

The next night I sat on the front steps on a particularly warm October night in 1998. Amanda drove up promptly at eight o'clock in her familiar beat up 1988 Oldsmobile Ninety-Eight Regency, scraping the passenger front tire against the curb as she stopped in front of the house. She was always a shitty driver. Brett was in the passenger seat. Amanda walked up to me with Brett watching my every move from the car.

"What is it?" She said, standing on the sidewalk in front of me. She crossed her arms over her breasts and was nervously bouncing to a rhythm the way women do when they are annoyed.

"I recently went through some stuff and I wanted to say I'm sorry. I know I'm a fucking idiot. You can call me whatever you want. But I just wanted to say I'm sorry for treating you the way I did."

"Is that all?"

"Basically."

"Am I supposed to accept your apology?" She sneered.

"Not really. If you want, that would be nice. I just want to say sorry." I stared up at her from the porch steps. She stared back as to challenge me to a contest. I looked over at Brett and he was still drilling holes into me with the laser beams coming from his eyes.

"This was a waste of time. Don't call me again." She turned and stomped off. Her sexy hips swayed like I remembered. *Brett's the lucky bastard now*. I watched her drive down the road and I started to feel much better. I did it more for myself than for her. When her Ninety-Eight disappeared down the block I was convinced that I did a good thing for myself. *Fuck her if she can't take a joke*, I thought, and went back inside and started getting ready for work.

12

Shortly after that little sour meeting, I got a job at a place just down the road from Westwood called Goulet Film. Westwood closed their doors and moved out of town a few years after I left and a ghost of a building is all that remains. Work at Goulet was mind numbing. I was their chip tester. I would hook up computer chips to this device that tested its current and I would record it. I was so emotionally fucked up I didn't care what I was doing anyway. I banged half the women there. *Not really*. I wasn't picky either. I started hanging out with a lady who was nine years older than me and I caught wind that she liked me. She was a round over-weight Italian woman. She didn't even look pretty. I didn't know what I was doing. When our shift was over we would go back to her place and she would let me use her computer which had America Online and really fast dial-up. She would buy me gifts and was not shy in letting me know I could have *whatever I wanted.*

One night she got me drunk on about five or six stiff vodka sours, and you know the rest. The next day, she commenced to tell me she had made an appointment to see her Gynecologist the following week to take a pregnancy test. She tried to trap me to no avail. It came back negative. Two months later, a friend of hers fresh out of prison, called her up looking for some action and she succeeded then. Poor bastard.

Sheri Cotton was a lady that worked at Goulet before I did. She started renting the upstairs apartment from my Dad and they soon started dating. Her hair was all white and she was about Dad's age, in her late fifties. She was a real cool cat. I used to enjoy having a few *totties* with her while she told stories of her times in Arizona and the musicians she knew there. I met her daughter Trina one night and she was as cool as her Mom. She was half Lebanese with long straight dark hair that stretched to the small of her back. For the most part she was a pretty woman except she had crooked teeth. She worked at the hospital in nearby Lewiston, sanitizing and assembling surgical kits. On Friday and Saturday nights she also tended bar at Johnny's Gin Mill in Donald Junction, where she lived, the town just north of Niagara Falls.

She rented a nice cozy bungalow in the nice section of town but barely scraped by. She offered to rent me a spare room for $300 a month. That was fine by me. I was bringing that home weekly at Goulet because they recently promoted me to Quality Inspector. Trina and I were fast friends.

Jackie Laurens was a girl I met at Goulet I brought back one night and Trina caught me sneaking her in. Trina met her and knew who she was. Jackie was a plain Native American girl with smooth skin and long, straight, jet black hair. She was a huge fan of music especially Guns N' Roses. I liked her the moment I met her.

"So this girl you had over last night, Shortman." Trina had her own nickname for me. "Are you boyfriend-girlfriend or just slammin partners?"

I cracked up. I never heard that before. "Slammin partners I guess... She just got divorced, and not looking for anything serious. Plus she has two kids, I'm not vibin on that."

Trina smiled, it showed her crooked front tooth. It was a slight imperfection. Slight imperfections on a woman make strange things happen south of my belt. "Well, be careful Shortman. We ladies get attached *QUICK*. Even if she says otherwise, sex means something to women." She made quotes with her index and middle fingers and said, "*Most* women."

"Well, she said she doesn't want anything serious."

"Just watch out. I'm looking out for ya."

She was good for advice even if I wasn't looking for any. It was like I had insider information on the opposite sex. "I'll keep that in mind."

Jackie and I had a deal. We were each other's fall back until one of us started dating someone new. And if that happened, the other would back away. I didn't listen to Trina. Jackie let me do whatever I wanted to her. You name it, she let me. After a night of drinking for free at Johnny's thanks to Trina, I would score a little coke, call up Jackie to meet me back at my room, and she would be waiting naked on my bed with left over lasagna in the microwave. We would fuck all night pausing only for me to snort a few lines off her ass.

13

The cloud of smoke hanging in the kitchen was so thick it looked like it was going to open up and rain. Dad was sitting at the breakfast bar with Sheri, sucking down cancer sticks, and watching MASH reruns. The television hung on the wall like a sad lonely beacon.

"What's going on?" I said.

"Hey Shorty." Sheri greeted.

"You two up to anything tonight?" I asked.

"Not really." Dad answered. "Did you hear?"

I braced. *Here we go again.* "What?"

"Mesha kicked out Junior." Sheri said. "He's on his way here."

"No way..." I sighed. At least no one is dead.

"Oh yeah." Dad said softly. He shot me a look that said *I'm not kidding.*

"Wow! What happened?"

Dad just shook his head. I couldn't believe what I was hearing. After Junior returned from the Air Force, he reconnected with a girl he knew from high school. Mesha was a smoking hot blond of Russian descent with a killer body and a personality that was so sweet you had no choice but to love her. They were supposed to grow old together. I walked to the fridge and helped myself to a silver bullet and sat down with Dad and Sheri.

"She can't take his drinkin." Dad confessed.

We didn't talk about the ramped alcoholism in our family. My sibling's mother was a fall down drunk who lived in an apartment complex for senior citizens downtown. She received food stamps and was unemployed for vast amounts of time. She also had horrible emphysema from years of smoking, which would eventually lead to her demise. At least my Dad functioned. Despite his alcoholism, he went to work and there were no creditors kicking in his doors. But this news started to make sense. One time Junior went to redeem his empty bottles, and after three trips to Tops Market, he had seventy-five dollars! That was 1500 bottles! I remember seeing this mountain of bottles thinking it was cool, never once thinking this man had a serious problem.

He was drinking a case of beer a day. We never saw this because he went to work every day and paid his bills, just like Dad. This was bad news. He had just graduated from the Police Academy and he was beyond excited living his lifelong dream of being a cop. We all were, but alcohol, a stressful job, and guns do not mix. I simply didn't realize what was going on, no one did except Mesha. I was blind to it. The entire family was blind to it.

Junior and I would meet up at around five or six o'clock in the evening at a place called Crazy Jim's and *prime up*. At around nine, we would split off to shower and get ready for a night of bar hopping and pool sharking. Our popular haunt after hours was a place called Rico's. We owned the pool table there. There was a taco shop that stayed open until four in the morning tending to all us drunk bastards that needed a bite to eat before we went home and crashed for the night. One night I was so drunk, Junior dropped me off in front of Trina's and while I fumbled with the keys to open the front door, I had put my burrito in my back pocket. I got to my room and passed out on the floor. The next morning Jackie showed up and Trina let her in as she always did. I was shaken awake by Jackie in a panic because I had slept on the burrito and it was smeared all over the floor and my clothes. She thought someone came in during the night and murdered me.

Junior's marriage was falling apart and the family contributed to it. Sure, he was the one in the marriage, but we all acted like nothing was wrong. We were cowards.

14

I was moved to the mold press at Goulet, which was stimulating my brain better than testing chips did, but pissed me off because I loved the Quality Technician job. One Monday night, Carla, a short squatty blonde who worked in Annealing, was giving a new temp a tour of the place. When they walked into the mold room, my life changed for the next ten years.

The new temp was short. Her hair was blonde but her brunette roots showed because she was growing it out to her original color. She wore brown corduroy pants that hugged her hips perfect. Her front teeth were jagged, but her lips were full and soft like inviting flower pedals.

"Hey Muffin!" Carla said. All the ladies at Goulet had a nickname for me. I had several nicknames like "Eye Candy", and "Sweet Cheeks". Carla was no different. She was an older married lady that loved the attention I gave her now and again, but would never dream of ruining her perfect marriage.

"Hey Carla, how you doing tonight baby? Busy over there in the clean room?"

"A little."

"I see they gave you a temp finally. Took them long enough."

"Tell me about it." She slyly leaned against my desk. I relished the attention I got there.

"Who do we have here?" I asked.

"This is Pamela." Carla said pointing in Pamela's general direction.

"Hi Pamela." I greeted.

"Hello." Her eyes were green and twinkled in the florescent lights over my desk.

"I like your song." I referenced to the Toto song. This was lost on her. She looked at me like I had six eyeballs.

"How's Shorty tonight?" Carla asked.

"I'll be ok. I have a few orders left tonight. I'm hoping to cruise through after midnight."

"Well, stop by if you get bored."

"Right on baby." I gave a wink to Pamela. "Nice meeting you Pam. My name's Shorty by the way."

"Oh, ok. You too Shorty."

I stared at her behind as she strutted away. *Just another bee in the hive.* I thought. Looking back, I wish it would have ended up that way.

15

One night at work I stopped by Annealing and asked Pamela to a movie. "American Psycho" was in theaters. Pamela was a sweet woman, but older than me by twelve years. Again, a lady going through a divorce, with three young kids. My entire family didn't like her because of those two facts alone. When we started dating, I broke off the "agreement" with Jackie. I wanted to keep everything honest. Two days later, Jackie walked over to my place and stuffed a four page letter in my mailbox. The letter went on about how we had something good, and she had fell in love with me. She wrote of the memories she will have, but didn't forget to tell me how upset she was with me and how used she felt. Four solid pages worth.

Trina was right. I felt like a complete shithead. I was so naïve to notice what had happened with Jackie. I never had those feelings for her. I was having fun, and that's all that mattered. I felt horrible.

Pam and I were moved into the clean room at work plating gold on computer chips. We started hanging out watching movies, and had common interests in eighties new wave and nineties grunge bands, as well as the TV show, "The X-Files". Things progressed well for a while. A month into our relationship I got a call from Jackie. She sounded shook up. I told her to meet me at my house after work.

"I'm pregnant."

"Shit." There was a long silence. "It's all good." I said. "I'll be there for everything. The doctor's appointments and everything. I'll help you take care of the baby."

"It's ok. You don't have to if you don't want to. We can have an abortion or I can take care of the baby all by myself. You don't have to be involved."

I'll be damned if another woman was going to have an abortion on my watch. That was out of the question. It was time to man up.

I hugged her. She was distraught. Dad taught me to take care of business. *TCB* he called it. *You get yourself in a situation, you handle it like a real man.* So I did. I held her close. I remember the scent of her shampoo was turning me on. We could have had sex. But I didn't want to ruin my relationship with Pam. She told me she had an appointment with her gyno in two weeks. I told her to call me when she needed me.

That night I met with Pam at The Gin Mill and told her the news. This upset her something awful and we almost broke up. We left and drove around the city talking about the situation. It was like I was talking to Trina. Pam told me how stupid I was, doing that to Jackie. *Women always get attached.* I had to convince her that night that our relationship was in no way like my relationship with Jackie. That was a chore. Pam didn't believe me for a second. Finally, deep into the night I had smoothed things over. I wish I hadn't.

That "pregnancy" turned out to be an adverse reaction to her birth control. Jackie moved to Nevada and married a teacher. She is happy and currently living happily ever after.

16

Dad's sister Janette came to visit from Pennsylvania that spring. Six months prior she found out she had cancer. Aunt Janette was the coolest woman I ever meet. She was sweet, down to earth, hysterically funny, and when she laughed it was loud and meaningful. She complained of a backache to her doctor while she was there for a routine checkup so they took an x-ray. Results came back positive. Non-operable tumor between her heart and lungs, thanks for playing. I believe that visit was her "Farewell" tour. She quit smoking when she found out but the damage was done. One night around two in the morning, Dad and I sat with Aunt Janette in the kitchen while she talked about their parents. Grandma Edna passed a few years prior in 1997, and Grandpa Alvin passed before I was born.

"I couldn't do what Dad did." Aunt Janette said.

"What, keep it secret?" Dad replied, leaning on the kitchen counter. A sweaty beer sat at his elbow.

"Yeah, I couldn't keep this from my kids."

"It was a different time Janette. And it's the Irish in us. Dad didn't want us to worry."

"It was so quick though. We found out on Halloween. He was dead on Thanksgiving. I never got over that. He was such a strong man."

She looked my way. "Dad had hands the size of frying pans Shorty!"

"I know. I've seen pictures." I could only imagine giving Grandpa a handshake. It probably would have been like shaking with a bunch of bananas. That's where Dad got his gigantic meat hooks.

She turned back to Dad. "How you holding up? I must be bringing back memories of Cora with my cancer and all."

Dad frowned and shook his head. "I'm fine, just worried about my little sister, that's all." Dad could keep up the tough guy routine. He was very good at it.

"How did you deal with that toward the end?" She

was running her fingers through the long snarly threads on the place mat in front of her.

"It was good for the most part. Every day I made sure she had the right medication and dosages. As long as I had it written down I was good. Those were the times I forgot she even had it."

"Yeah, I'm know what you mean." She said.

"Only at the very end it got tough." Dad continued. "Her demeanor changed. It was like she gave up. One morning I got her medication together and she didn't want to take it cause of how it was making her look, all the steroids were puttin weight on her. So we were arguin about all that. I told her she had to keep takin her medication. She said, 'Yeah? You want me to take my medication?' and she threw all her pills in her mouth and started chewing. Some fell on the floor, pieces were fallin out her mouth, soggy pills on her lips. I didn't know what she had took or what, to get everything straight again. I didn't want to give the wrong medication or overdose her, so I went and called Hospice." He called it *Hospit.* "There was nothing I could do anymore."

"Damn Dad." I chimed in. "I didn't know that."

"Boy, did she give me a glare when they sat her up on the gurney to take her away." He whistled. "She glared at me the entire time till they rolled her away. She knew she wasn't coming back to the house."

"That's a hard thing to do." Aunt Janette said. "I will never forget the last few days with Dad, how hard it was."

"Laurie, her sister came in from out of town to be with her the last few days. Her last night, the doctors knew it was close so they let us stay, visiting hours didn't apply anymore." He started fiddling with the beer, twisting it until the mouth of the can faced him. "Cora was sleeping in a fetal position. She sat up and looked around," Dad demonstrated, "she had gone blind, her irises had gone white and cloudy. Me and Laurie looked at each other, Cora turned and laid back down. Then she exhaled." Dad exhaled, driving the moment home. Dad choked just then, his eyes watery. "I put my hand by her mouth to feel her breath but she was gone."

A tear streamed down both cheeks just then. His jaw quivered then stopped. That was the second and last time I saw my Dad cry. Aunt Janette sensed him suck it back in like our family does.

"Oh, there's nothing wrong with cryin every now and then. It's good for you. It feels good." Aunt Janette told him.

"I haven't thought of that in years." Dad replied. "You know I coulda had her buried next to your mother?" He said to me. "There was a plot open. There was no way I was gonna do that. So I put her across the street." He joked, she was actually across the path from the family plots. He had forgotten I was with him the day to make arrangements for the burial.

Maybe Dad was a little hard because two wives had died on his watch. I can't imagine what that is like. But I was still a selfish dickhead that didn't think of anyone but myself. I wasn't seeing the whole picture just yet.

17

Pam was real cool at first. She would hang out with Junior and me and witness first hand all our debauchery. Junior and his wife were trying to give their marriage one last shot while Pam was trying to get me to ease up on my partying lifestyle.

"Hey brother." I said standing next to Junior one Friday. I had just got off the clock, working as a maintenance man at the time for a guy who owned a bunch of properties all over Donald Junction. We were at a place called Carlyle's Tavern and Motel. It was a dirty place that smelled like old people and musk. The stuff on the walls consisted of yellowing posters of old Bills and Yankees game schedules mostly from the 1970's, and newspaper clippings of various neighborhood happenings. It had a string of six rooms off to the left of the building that posed for the "and Motel" in the name. But they were hardly that. Those rooms were reserved for drunks that were kicked out of their homes by their old ladies who finally had the courage to do it. They smelled of mold and vomit.

"Yo!" Junior answered. He knew I was coming. We planned the meeting. "I ordered you a frosty one." A cold beer sat sweating next to him on the bar. "Marriage is done. It's all over."

"Damn dude, that sucks." I bellied up to the bar. I knew what happened. He got caught cheating with a badge bunny he knew from uptown. He didn't know I knew, but Niagara Falls is a small town. News traveled fast. "I'm sorry man."

"It's all good. I couldn't help myself. I was gonna stop all the shit and give it an honest shot but I didn't. Because I'm weak."

He was always honest with me. We'll be bros to the end me and Junior. Just the way it's going to be.

"People make mistakes. Just pull up your socks and

keep moving." I could not believe that actually came out of my mouth.

"Fuck don't say that." He said sharply. "I can't stand it when Dad says it." He then signed quotes with his hands and said, *pull up your socks*, mocking Dads voice. I chuckled. I couldn't believe I just said that.

"We hate that phrase but he's right, that crotchety bastard."

"I know." Junior agreed.

Just then my cell phone rang and Pam's number lit up the little screen. "Hey baby, what's the plan?"

"Want to come over? I'm making homemade manicotti." She asked.

"Wow! That sounds great." I answered.

Junior overheard the conversation. "Really?!? You're blowing me off for a piece of ass?" He scolded. He forgets so easily the million times he has done it to me.

"What did he say?" Pam asked.

"Nothing. Give me twenty minutes to finish my beer and I'll be over."

"Ok."

I hung up and noticed Junior was livid. "I can't fuckin believe you." He threw his hands up.

"What? I'm just having dinner, I'll meet up with you later. Let's have a few beers and break a few racks on the felt over there." I pointed at the pool table, it was open as always.

"Don't fuckin bother, just go over there to your trim. I'll see you later."

"Fuck dude, are you gonna be like that?"

"I would never do that to you. Matter of fact, I gotta go."

He left a dollar on the bar next to his half full mug of Bud draft and stormed out. I sat sipping my beer. I shook my head counting the times he blew me off for some girl a year back. I didn't count the times he laughed at me leaving me with a woman who was not desirable to put it nice, as I struggled to get away from her advances because I was too nice of a guy to tell her I wasn't interested.

After he left, Bob Seger started singing "Night Moves" from the jukebox that was in the corner. I slugged the last of my Bud, pulled a single from my pocket, slid it under the mug and left the bar dreaming of manicotti.

18

For two years things were nice. Our relationship had its ups and downs. She helped me get straight. Right from the beginning she said she wouldn't date a smoker, a heavy drinker, or a drug user. I was all three, and I stopped all that for her cold turkey. I took her to meet my grandfather and she watched Yankees games with us. She hated baseball, but she liked Grandpa. She would bring food over for us to eat when we watched ballgames. Things like this went on for a while and it was really nice. But cracks started to show. She wanted to keep tabs on me for everything, which was understandable due to her past relationships ending by unfaithful counterparts.

One night I was checking my e-mail and I received one from a good looking girl named Andrea. The e-mail said she met me a few months earlier at Johnnies. Trina had introduced us.

"Do you know a girl named Andrea?" I asked Trina one night while she worked. "You apparently introduced us one night. She's cute, redhead?"

"No. I don't know any Andreas." Trina answered as she wiped off the bar. "I would remember introducing you. Who is this chick??"

"I got an e-mail from this girl named Andrea. Says she knows you." I shrugged.

Trina dried off rocks glasses with a fresh rag. She was prideful in her work. She would arrange the beer cooler or clean a dirty toilet with the same attention to detail. "No. I don't know anyone named Andrea."

"Strange… thought I'd ask."

"Go out with her." Trina said. She raised her hand like a student that wanted to be called up to the blackboard. "Pam is not the chick for you."

"I hear that a lot." I drained my Molson Canadian and set it on the inside edge of the bar.

"You don't listen a lot." She laughed. She took the empty bottle and put it in a case holding other dead soldiers under the bar.

"You're so funny." I mocked back at her.

"What's it gonna hurt? You want to kick Pam to the curb anyway."

"So you don't know her."

"No, I don't know any Andrea's." Trina sobered.

"Weird."

Later that night, I replied to the e-mail writing although I was flattered by her interest, I was having difficulty with my current relationship and it wouldn't be fair to her to involve her right now. Andrea replied saying she respected my reply and wished me luck with my current situation. I didn't want to cheat and lie anymore. Covering up a lie is such a chore. That's what that was all about really.

Things between Pam and I smoothed out and we kept on rolling. I enrolled in college again that spring after a few semesters away. During finals week, Pam and I again were on the outs, when I received another e-mail from Andrea. I looked at her yahoo profile, as I did the previous time she contact me. She was a nice thin redhead, with blue eyes, and an undying love for her orange tabby named Henri. The e-mail said,

Hello, how you doing? How's life? I just wanted to check and see if you were still in a relationship, and if not, can we go out for a drink?

So I replied this time,

My relationship is dead, (I had planned on breaking up with Pam that night) **I would love to have a drink with you. Meet me at Johnnies tonight?**

Her reply,

I can't wait

That afternoon after my Art History final, which despite my artistic abilities, I couldn't stand but it was required, I walked down the hall to the parking lot door. I saw Pam walking up the hall toward me. *This would be perfect.* I thought. *We can go to lunch, I can break up with her without her making a scene in public, and we could go our separate ways*. She had other plans.

"Hey, surprised to see you here. I thought maybe we could got to lunch. I have to ta--"

"We don't have to talk about anything." She fumed. She had a stack of papers in her hand and she threw them at me. "There is no Andrea. I made her up."

"WHAT?!?"

"Yeah, her profile bio, everything. Even her cat Henri. You chased a figment of my imagination."

"Why did you go through all this trouble, just break up with me? You're nuts." I said.

"I wanted to see if you would bite on it."

I looked at her puzzled. "Six months you played this charade."

She started walking away. "Pick up your things, I want you out by tonight." She said talking over her shoulder.

"Sounds good to me, I was going to break up with you at lunch anyway."

"Right." She relied sarcastically.

Wow, I thought. *Six months she had this on the line. She is certified crazy town. That is some crazy, crazy, shit.* I picked up the papers at my feet. They were all the emails back and forth between "Andrea" and me. She had her own e-mail address and a lovely bio about how she loved her job and hanging out with friends and blah, blah, blah. Unbelievable.

I threw the papers in the trash can outside, and started driving home. I couldn't help but laugh at what would come to be known as "The Andrea Incident." I guess I brought out the crazy in her. I should have seen the red flag at that point, but I didn't. I drove to Dads to tell him the news and ask if I could crash upstairs for a while. He thought it was the funniest thing he ever heard. Tears of a different variety streamed down his face. I called Junior and asked him to come with me when I picked up my things. When we arrived, Pam had neatly put my things in the living room for me to pick up. That was one of the few times my stuff was in a nice neat pile to pick up when she kicked me out.

One time I spent an all-nighter drinking with Junior and when we walked up to the house the next morning, I walked past my 1988 Chevy Caprice in the driveway and noticed all my stuff packed in it. Junior immediately fell out. He said the look on my face was priceless. He still talks about that to this day. Another time I was trying to leave Pam in the middle of the day and move all my stuff by the time she came home from work. But I didn't plan on her coming home at lunch time to check the mail and caught me red handed like a thief in the night. She commenced to tell me to get the fuck out. When I came back for the rest of my things about forty-five minutes later, she had thrown all my things in the front yard. Dad and I gathered them up as fast as we could while the whole neighborhood watched on intently at the events that unfold.

19

One day I got a dividend check in the mail from Mellon Investors for three dollars and some change. I didn't have any investments that I knew off so I called them. After I gave them the account number on the statement, the guy on the other end told me it was from a life insurance policy that was recently closed out due to twenty years of non-activity. I thanked him for his time and then I called Dad.

131

"So I got this check in the mail from Mellon Investors today. I didn't understand where it came from so I called them."

"What they say?" Dad asked.

"They said, there was a life insurance policy that Ma set up for me care of you."

"Oh yeah. I remember."

"They said you closed out the account in 1983, and this check was all that was left."

"How much?"

"Three dollars and eighty-two cents."

"That's yours. Go buy a beer with it."

"Where's this money. It was mine. I was supposed to get it when I was twenty-one according to the policy."

"I needed it. And you did get it. You had clothes on you back and food in your belly."

"And apparently a year-long vacation upstate and a mega Christmas for everyone in 1983." In 1984, we lived in Malone, New York in a huge mansion of a house. It was one uneventful year until we moved back to Niagara Falls. Now I know who paid the bill.

"Oh Shorty relax."

"I could have used that money for college. I wouldn't have to struggle with student loans. Did you ever think of that?"

"You didn't starve, you ever think of that?"

"Fuck it!" I said and hung up on him. I was livid. This guy was constantly robbing me and it was getting old. I didn't talk to him for three months hoping to get an apology from him but I never got one. I was more likely to grow a

fucking horn out of my forehead than get an apology from
my father.

20

A few months before a group of foreigners from the
Middle East crashed planes into the Twin Towers, I started
having a reoccurring nightmare. I think it was because my
relationship with Pam wasn't going so smooth. It never went
that great to be honest. We had periods of good times but
they never lasted too long. Pam would belittle me a lot,
especially in front of her friends. She was now in the habit of
telling me I was a bum for not holding down a job any time
she had the chance. Her ex-husband cheated on her with a
co-worker and this contributed to her lack of trust toward
men, and "The Andrea Incident" didn't help my cause. She
checked my cell phone all the time and asked about any
number out of the ordinary. She treated me like a kid.

My déjà vu fits didn't help the situation either. I was
having two a month like clockwork. They weren't as long as
the ones I had in 1995. They would last twenty seconds, then
fade away. Really weird stuff. But the fear was still
crippling as ever. I wouldn't wish these feelings on my worst
enemy.

This nightmare was, for a lack of a better term,
fucked up beyond belief. It was tough to talk about over the
years because of what happened in it. But it was a
nightmare. Crazy things happen in nightmares. Crazy,
crazy, things.

I'm walking through the back door on Sixty-Fifth
Street. There was clutter everywhere, which is strange

because Dad kept the house clean due to his spartan discipline. He was not home.

"Dad." I called. I walked through the kitchen to the dining room. "Dad!" I called again, my voice echoed through the house. There were large cracks that sprawled down the walls. A light was on in his bedroom. I walked to the light that shined through the doorway; my feet heavy as cinder blocks. My heart stopped; I'm frightened to death to see Cora sitting with her back to the bed hugging her bare knees to her chest. She's crying with her head resting on her knees.

"Wha...What are you doing here?!? You're dead...you are not here." She looked up with her cheeks soaked with tears. I smelled fresh earth.

"Why are you doing this to me?" She asked. "I loved you Shorty. I've always loved you. Why?" She wore a dirty shirt wet with mud.

"WHAT?!?" I shouted, "Why did you do this TO ME?!? I WAS JUST A KID!! I smacked her across the face and it echoed through the bedroom. I would never hit a woman.

"You loved it you horny little bastard. You're gay as the night is long. But you loved to get an eyeball full of my PUSSY!!!" Her face twisted and contorted. Tears streamed down to her filthy shirt. Her eyelids had angry red circles around them.

"FUCK YOU! YOU ARE NOT HERE!!!" I yelled and pushed her down on her stomach. She cried harder, face down in the carpet.

"Why, Shorty? Why are you doing this?" She cried. I got on top of her and punched the back of her head. I reeled back and gave her two shots between her shoulder blades.

"You're not here. You're dead. SHUT THE FUCK UP!" I went out of my mind. "YOU ABUSED ME FOR YEARS THIS IS WHAT YOU GET!" She tried to buck me off of her like she was a stallion but my pelvis just slammed back down on her butt. Her underwear were smudged with mud. She tried to buck me off again, and her shirt flew up around her shoulders. I rained punches on her. "You teased me for years. THIS IS WHAT YOU GET!" I shouted.

I reached down and pulled her panties to her thighs, snapping the band in half. Her butt was covered with sweat.

"BITCH!" I yelled.

"NO! DON'T!!" She sobbed. She tried to fight with me but I had the leverage. There was no hesitation. I pulled my shorts down and slammed my penis in her. Her tune changed.

"WHORE! YOU DESERVE THIS!" I blasted.

"GIVE IT TO ME YOU SICK FUCK, YOU UNHOLY DEPRAVED BASTARD!" I kept slamming. The rage and hate boiled in me. I was possessed. I wanted to hurt her and this was the ultimate way to do it. I wanted to hurt her so deep. I wanted to break her. She started to laugh loud and deviously.

"SHUT UP!" I screamed, tears streaming from my eyes.

"I LIKE IT UP THE ASS. YOU CAN'T HURT ME YOU LITTLE FAGGOT!" She egged on. I was punching her, I smashed down fists on her spine. I vigorously started blasting my pelvis in her as hard as I could. She screamed and laughed.

"FUCKING SLUT! STOP LAUGHING!! I'LL GIVE YOU SOMETHING TO SCREAM ABOUT!"

I woke screaming lurching forward in bed, my heart slamming out of my chest. My side of the bed, sheets, pillow, blanket, would be drenched in sweat. Pamela threw an arm around me to hold me back as I writhed around.

"BREATHE Shorty. Breathe... It was just a dream." She comforted. "Just a dream..." Her arm slid off my chest from the sweat. Still disorientated, I threw my legs over the side of the bed to get up but I fell to the floor. They felt like rubber bands. I was gasping for air like I just held my breath under water for the last ten minutes. The gasps were coming out *HI, HE, HE, HI*. Pam ran around the bed to my side of the floor.

"It's ok. I'm here." She dropped down on her knees and threw her arms around my head. "Relax." She said softly. "Relax." She started stroking my head smoothly. My hair was matted down with moisture. "Easy." She whispered. "Breathe...Take it easy."

After the disorientation, I faded and fell asleep on the floor in the dark with my head in Pamela's lap.

I woke up the next morning with a feeling of disgust. I didn't want to face Pam or anyone in the world. It's a deep disgust I can't explain. I wanted to spend a week in the shower.

"So what was that about last night?" Pamela asked. I bet it scared the shit out of her as much as it did me.

"I can't remember." I lied. "I can't remember it now."

21

One day after class, I was greeted by Dad and Sheri sitting in a row at the breakfast bar in the kitchen, fresh frosty silver bullets in front of them.

"Did you hear?" Dad asked.

"What."

"David Bones, dead!" Dad sucked on a cigarette and a large plume of smoke engulfed his head.

"Jesus! I just saw him a few weeks ago. He invited us to the park to celebrate his daughter's birthday, told me to say hi to the sisters."

"Well, I just talked to Denny, his funeral is this weekend."

"Wow. I can't believe it." I mumbled. "I wonder if they're gonna let Mack out of jail to attend." I had learned through the grapevine he had been in county lockup the past two months on charges of petite theft, and breaking and entering. Since the last time we spoke, he had been in and out of jail for stupid little things, like vandalism and disturbing the peace. I liked to party, but I never wanted to end up in jail. I hung out with him less often while he started hanging out with a group of ravers and ecstasy poppers in Buffalo. He understood I wasn't about that.

"Denny had to bail him out of jail. Can you imagine what he's going through? He has to bury one son, and another he's bailing out of jail to attend the funeral. He said he wasn't having Mack at the funeral in an orange jumpsuit and handcuffs so he coughed up the bread to spring him."

"Jesus, how is Denny holding up?"

"Barely, I would be too. I've known David since he

was shittin yellow." He took a large gulp from his beer. "I said you and Junior will be pall bearers."

"Of course, I would be honored."

"Mack's home, you should give him a call."

I did give Mack a call later that night. He was in a bad way of course. He talked about David, and the memories he had. He was a tall fit man due to his football playing days in high school. He always took care of his physique the same way he took care of his family. He was a true family man.

I couldn't imagine losing a brother and the hurt he felt. I did not see him until the funeral service. We didn't need to catch up on the last few years we didn't hang out. We were best friends. It happened by itself. I cried at David's funeral, more for the pain the Bones family was going through. He was a dear family friend. We were all second generation friends. It tore up Mack and his family. Mack's other brother Kory, a mountain of a man also due to decades of gym hours, lost it when they closed David's coffin for the last time. I will never forget the sound of his sobs.

David had a prescription for morphine patches because of his back problems due to a car accident he was involved in back in his teens. The coroner found two patches on his arm, and two rolled up in his stomach. Good night sweet prince.

You would think David's death would serve as a cruel omen to Mack, but of course, he didn't stop using drugs so we went back to our lives as they were before the funeral. He had court dates to wade through because periodically I would see his name in the paper for various boneheaded things. He once stole a car and was caught painting it in his driveway at two in the morning. The cops showed up and there were spray cans strewn all over his front yard. It must have been quite a sight to be seen.

22

I was back in school again, for the third time. One day I was enjoying a tasty plate of chicken parmigiana in the cafeteria when I saw Amanda's friend Mary. She was around every now and again back in high school. She hung out in the background. We decided to have lunch together every Thursday due to our class schedules being so similar that day of the week. One day I just launched into it.

"So you still hang out with Amanda?" I asked.

Mary was a shy girl unless she knew you. She looked at me through her bright red curls. Her hair was the color of Raggedy Ann's. She was more attractive than she was in high school. "Yeah. Why you ask?"

"You think she would talk to me? You know we had a falling out four years ago."

"You're her kryptonite Shorty. You know that. She can never stay mad at you. I think she will." Mary replied. She shot me a look, *here we go again*. She knew the various ins and outs of the relationship that was Amanda and Shorty.

"Give her my number?"

She gave a hard sigh. "Yeah, I suppose."

"What?"

She played with a curl that was just behind her left ear. "You know what. I know where this is going."

"What are you talking about?" I smirked at her. "I just want to have things right between us that's all. Really." I had anterior motive. She saw right through it.

Later that evening, Amanda called me and we made plans to hang out at my dad's house. She had lost weight since I saw her last. But other than that she was the same old Amanda. We talked of her relationship with Brett which just ended after six years, and my debacle with Pamela, which was on again.

"I just wanted to say I'm sorry. Why didn't you accept my apology that night I called you over?"

"I was still mad at you. That hurt." She had shorter hair, but had enough to twirl around her index finger.

"I was trying to iron all that out the best I could." I reiterated.

"I know. It was a secret. Between me and you… and it hurt me. But that's all in the past."

"Good. I'm glad. We can be friends again?"

"Sure." We sat in silence for about fifteen, twenty seconds. "So are we going to do this?" She said as she started unbuttoning her blouse. She was wearing a red bra. I had forgotten how great her rack was. I don't recall her being this forward.

"Uh... Yeah." I was caught off guard. Usually I was the one that charmed the pants off the ladies.

"This is what this is right?" She slipped off her pants and they hit the floor. She had lost the weight proportionately. All my senses came alive. There was no turning back. "Since you have a girlfriend. I'm completely ok with being the 'other girl'".

"You don't have to ask me twice."

We were back at it again. We always had great sex and this was no different. The next time I called her for some action, I picked her up at a party she was not enthusiastic about being at. She commended me on my perfect timing. The last time we had sex, she showed up naked from the waist down wearing just a pink lace nightie under her winter coat. She gave me a blow job while I was saying good night to Pam on the phone.

Three years later, in the summer of 2005, Amanda tracked me down on Myspace. We planned to *pick up where we left off.* When she arrived she said she couldn't do it anymore. She was dating a guy she found online and said she couldn't cheat on him. She then promptly moved to where he lived and cut me off. That was the last I spoke to her. I think that was her way of cutting the ties, her way, for the last time. Good riddance.

Amanda Kurtz now lives in Raleigh, North Carolina with the engineer she met online. They have a daughter together and she refuses to talk to me or my wife. She currently lives a mere fifty miles from us.

23

I drove up Dad's driveway one afternoon on an unseasonably warm March day in 2003. Jerald, Petrisha's first born, was standing in the back yard in cargo shorts, wearing sandals and white tube socks. His blond hair was buzzed to the scalp and still shaped his facial hair into a goatee fresh from 1992.

"You look Canadian." I told him as I exited my truck.

"Guess what Unc!" He exclaimed.

"You bought a new shirt?" I joked, pointing out the wing sauce stains.

"I'm gonna be a Daddy." He said, sucking on his cigarette.

I was ecstatic for him… Really. But I felt a twinge of jealousy. Even though I wasn't ready, and I KNEW Jerald wasn't ready by a LONG SHOT being perpetually unemployed with no health benefits, I wanted kids. I thought I was supposed to beat him to it. But I was wrong. "That's awesome brother! Let's celebrate!"

"I'm so happy." He told me. "We wanted to wait until we knew it would stick to tell everyone."

"I'm excited for you!" I gave him a hug, probably our first ever. We are a family of non-huggers.

"We're having a girl and I want you to be her Godfather." I was shocked to say the least. "I know you're Atheist, but I know you will teach her all the options and point her to the right path. Whatever religion she chooses in her life."

"I'd be honored. Pick out any names yet?"

"Angelina Rose." He took a long drag from his Marlboro.

"Aw, that's beautiful man." I said. "I can't wait to meet her."

He stood there in the grass, his body shook with excitement and nervousness. He radiated. You could feel his anticipation for being a father. I knew he would be great at it, ready or not, and I stood there and envied him. "You should quit smoking. You'll teach her bad habits."

"I know. I'm tryin here." He said with a smile.

I put my arm around his shoulder and we headed toward the house to have a celebratory beer. I knew I would be a good Godfather. Regardless of what I believed, Jerald knew I would not influence her to go in any particular direction. I had researched religion and cosmology equally. I think another reason that I do not have any use for God and religion is that some years ago I was with Mack and his father driving home from the Festival of Lights. The Festival of Lights was a beautiful light display in Hyde Park that the City of Niagara Falls put up every Christmas season. Every year we would drive downtown in the crisp winter night to drive through the park and enjoy the sights.

So driving home on this particular trip, Denny making conversation says, "Hey guys, do you know why the stars sparkle?"

We looked out the car windows and gazed at the canopy of stars that were out that night. During a crisp, cold, and clear winter's night, there are billions in the sky.

"I dunno." Replied Mack.

"No." I added.

"It's because they reflect the light from the sun." He said.

I was always fascinated with the sky. That was what Denny knew, and he was trying to teach us something he only knew how. He didn't know that like our own Sun, which is indeed the closest Star to Planet Earth, the stars in the sky that night and any other night were shining because they are in fact balls of gas just like our star. Physics and Cosmology make a lot more sense to me than Religion and always has. Angelina Rose would be in good hands, whatever she chose to believe in the future.

24

After class one afternoon in April, I came home and
Dad was in the back laundry room sucking down a cancer
stick. He recently painted the interior of house and was
disgusted with himself because of the brown tobacco film he
had to cover. So the laundry room became his smoking area.

"Did you hear?" *Bad news.*

"What?" I asked reluctantly.

"Finn Markey, dead."

"What?!?" I exclaimed. "What happened to him?"
Finn worked with Dad and was Sonya's age. They went to
high school together, *Finnmeister* we called him. He played
drums and was a diehard Dolphins fan. He was a friend of
mine. I've bumped many lines with this guy. It's what we
were doing the last I seen of him.

"Drugs."

"Geez."

"He disappeared at work. He ran out of sick days, so
I called him to tell him I couldn't cover for him anymore. I
didn't get him so I called his mother." He crushed his Doral
out in the ashtray in front of him. "She drove to his place
and found him layin in his recliner. She thought he was
sleepin, so she tried to wake him, and he was dead. Autopsy
will come back in a month."

"That's a shame. He was such a cool dude. I've
jammed with him a few times."

"Well he won't need his drums anymore. What a
shame. Dead of stupidity."

I was shocked. He was a good dude. One night back
when I was living with Sonya at our apartment, she went out
partying and brought back a gaggle of people. Finnmeister
woke me up out a sound sleep, shoved a dented beer can in

my face and said, "SHORTY, come join us. I got a beer for you, it's still cold." So I did. We had a blast that night.

His autopsy found that he had taken a bunch of aspirins for a headache or who knows what. They thinned his blood, causing a clot in his leg to break free and end up in his lungs causing an embolism. He was thirty-six. I learned quickly from David Bones and now Finnmeister that no matter what you think, you're only immortal for a small window of time. They were good buddies and I miss them deeply.

But that wasn't the end of the bad news train. I saved the best for last. A few months later, I want to say it was a dreary morning. But it wasn't. It was grey and the sun was poking through the clouds in patches in the way it does in November with the cold snows of Western New York well on their way. Angelina was born two months prior so things were joyful for a change. It was good despite the crisp weather.

A partner and I recently started a construction business. We bid on a contract to build garages, decks, patios, any addition really, for Dreams Limited Modular Homes and got it. It was a sweet deal. The company was throwing us $25 a square foot to build these structures. My partner and I were rolling in the bread. We did this for two years until one Friday morning I forgot my work boots and stepped on a rusty nail. I went to the hospital to get a tetanus shot for precaution and told my partner I would be taking the rest of the day off. I called him the next morning to talk business.

Saturday morning came and he told me he somehow pissed off Dreams Limited and Sears (who were paying us

$350 a square to install vinyl siding), in the span of eight hours while I was at the hospital and lost both contracts. It was seventy-five percent of our business. I promptly quit after a heated dispute. He bought out my half and I walked away. Six months later, he ran the business into the ground. This turn of events was three months away.

Getting back to that November morning, I was driving by the wheat in Sanborn. My Tim Horton's coffee was just the right temperature, with a pinch of caramel flavoring and tasted perfect. It was going to be a good day. It was Tuesday. My partner and I were almost done with this garage build I was driving to and Dreams Limited had a sweet two tier deck job lined up for us to start on Monday. "Plowed" by Sponge was on the radio and I was thinking of how much I liked that song.

My cell phone rang and Pam's number lit up the face.

"Hey baby. You miss me already?"

"Shorty, you might wanna pull over." It didn't sound like her. She had been crying. It wasn't good. When someone says, *you might want to sit down*, or *you might want to pull over*, you know your day, possibly week or even longer, is about to get smashed to the ground.

I pulled over to the side of the road. "Ok. I'm stopped. What is it?"

I wasn't ready for it.

"Your grandfather..." She sobbed. She didn't need to finish. I already knew. "...he passed away early this morning. Your Uncle just called me with the news." She continued. "I'm so sorry Shorty. I'm so sorry."

The air escaped me and I couldn't breathe. "AWE NO." I howled into the phone. That was all I could muster.

I was beyond a loss for words. That heavy feeling you get in your chest when a loved one dies had settled in, and it was currently sinking through my stomach. Sure, losing friends hurt, but a loved one like a grandfather was all together a hurt in a league of its own. All of a sudden, Sponge didn't sound so good. My coffee didn't taste so sweet. And the day got a whole lot darker.

When I arrived back home, Pam stood in the kitchen doorway. She ran over and hugged me. I grunted in pain as tears poured from my eyes. Grandpa was my best friend, a man's man. A guy I could watch ball games with and he would laugh at me when I talked about various amusing things going on in my life. His apartment was a sanctuary. A get away from Cora when she was alive. I forgot about the world and my problems while I sat on his couch and watched the Yankees. Sometimes we sat in silence. Now he was gone, no I will miss you, no final good luck and goodbye.

He was late in flipping his calendar from October to November. While rehanging it standing on a chair from the kitchen, he fell, breaking his arm. After a few days in the hospital, the doctors were setting up dates for therapy in the spring and planned to release him. During the night, for whatever reason, his health deteriorated. He died fittingly on Veterans Day, November 11, 2003. He was seventy-seven.

I wasn't ready.

His funeral arrangements and service was a blur. I arrived drunk as a sailor at his wake. And when it was over, I bought a bottle of Jameson on the ride home. Pam didn't approve but didn't dare to say anything different. Sometimes after a three day bender with Mack while I was living with Grandpa, I would stumble in and flop on the couch and drift to sleep in the sun while he sat in his chair and watched baseball. Sometimes I would think about how safe and warm I felt at those moments. I will never forget them.

25

Shortly after I started having these late night drunk fests on the back deck. My friends were dead, my grandpa had just died, and I was feeling truly alone. Captain Morgan and Johnnie Walker were great company.

I would play CD's on my old radio and think about things in the stillness. One night, the radio station I listened to, *103.3 The Boneyard, Donald Junctions Rock Station playing hits from the 80's, 90's, and Today!*, played a song that I never heard on the radio. It was "Still Remains" by Stone Temple Pilots, mine and Miriam's song. I wallowed in self-pity. She was married with two kids last I heard and I was without a doubt, the furthest thing from her mind. I sat and slammed Johnny Walker like it was Kool-Aid, thinking about Miriam. She was the one that got away. I would be truly alone without her, and she was happy without me.

Darkness settled in and it got darker every time I had these late night pity parties. I thought of everyone, Sierra, Amanda, and Mack. I worried for Mack because of his lifestyle. I think he will be dead before he's thirty-five. I believe these times were the darkest I ever felt and the storm was at its peak. But again, I was wrong.

26

"Hey."

"Hey. I wanted to let you know I'm on the I-77, I crossed into North Carolina about five minutes ago, and I'm about two hours away." I say into my iPhone.

"I'm so excited. I can't believe you're doing this."

"Me either."

"I know. I just can't believe you're leaving your life behind for me like this. This is CRAZY." She whispers *crazy*. It sounds creepy.

"Yeah, it is."

"You can turn back." The voice offers.

"Not on your life. You're stuck with me now."

"I'm ok with that."

"Me too."

"I love you." The voice says.

"I love you too. More than you will ever know."

I break connection and keep my eyes on the road. I can't contain my excitement. I am two hours away. It is seven o'clock in the evening and the twilight grows. The summer sun is still over the horizon, and it looks much more beautiful here in North Carolina than in New York. I know it's because of where I am in life at this exact moment. Right before I crossed the Virginia-North Carolina border a few miles back, driving out of the mountains in a low cloud cover that is eye level, North Carolina stretched below in a sort of valley, and I will never forget that sight.

North Carolina is beautiful this time of year. The heat of the day still lingers but is losing to the dusk. It reminds me of when I was a boy and I would look out front door of our house on Sixty-Fifth Street and the sun was setting over the I-190 on a warm summer evening. The breeze would come through the screen door; I can still feel it.

It would bring in aromas of flowers and fresh cut grass from the front yard. My sister Sonya would be on the couch banging her gums on the phone with one of her friends while watching and listening to scrambled music videos on MTV. Scrambled videos like "Live to Tell" by Madonna, "These Dreams" by Heart, "Time After Time" by Cindi Lauper, and "I'm on Fire" by Bruce Springsteen.

I'm having that exact feeling right now. I know I belong here with her.

I know this is where I need to be.

There are certain things you know you just have to do. I just needed a nudge. I look in my rearview mirror to check if my load had shifted and everything is still golden. It is dark now, and all I see are periodic sets of red tail lights and sporadic green traffic signs being illuminated by headlights of wayward travelers such as myself. I wonder if any of these travelers are doing something as crazy and spontaneous as I am. What is their story? Are they just coming home from a long Monday at work? Will there be a beautiful loved one meeting them at the end of their trip? Are they just going for a drive to enjoy the warm night wind?

I can't help but think the storm I went through was meant for me to come to this moment stronger than I have ever been. I wish Grandpa was here to see where I am now in life. He taught me so much. My relationship with Dad had ups and downs but I understand why he is the way he is, *I understand.*

I drive in the dark with the sets of red tail lights. My excitement is stellar.

PART III
THE FALLING DARKNESS
AND THE AFTERMATH

1

Personally, to tell you the truth, it was convenient. I was jobless and my student loans were in default. Those were the reasons why I stayed with Pam. I thought I loved her. That's why I originally proposed to her on Christmas Eve in 2005. Sure, she had three kids and she treated me like her fourth, but we were on the same wave length for most of the time. Our favorite pastime was staying up way past midnight, drinking wine, and talking about our favorite bands or songs that reminded us of a moment in time. She was almost as big of a music snob as me. I thought she was the one.

2

Junior and his wife finalized their divorce that summer. He seemed ecstatic, talking about freedoms and being himself again. I knew better; he missed her plenty. His drinking didn't let up. He started using his vacation time during days of good weather. To add insult to injury, his soon-to-be ex-wife was accepted into the academy and was a cop by the end of the year. I believe this is where the spiral started.

Junior and a detective buddy he knew on the force went in together and bought Carlyle's which had spiraled into an abyss of debt. I heard through the grapevine the owner sold it to them for cheap. Junior dreamed of us owning a bar named "The Irish Duo." His dream had come true. I was happy because I could have a free drink every now and again. They turned that place stinking of stale booze and mold, into a happening sports bar with various paraphernalia on the walls complete with no less than eight televisions tuned in to various sports programs. It was an immediate hit with the locals.

"Hey, brother man." Junior said when I walked into "The Duo." It was a busy, early Friday evening. He sat at the corner of the bar with various customers.

"Hey. How's the force?" He hadn't been there the past few days.

"Good, can't complain." He shrugged. He swallowed half his Budweiser in one gulp.

"Business?"

"Fantastic!"

"Hey, Rhonda," I said to the barmaid, "what're you two up to tonight?"

"Nothin spectacular." She was the typical barfly we all know and love from a time or another in our lives. She was Junior's new girlfriend and enabler. It was starting to show on him.

"You got the place lookin nice." The place looked fresh. Football banners hung on the walls. Long gone teams like the Houston Oilers, St Louis Cardinals, and the Los Angeles Rams were hanging behind the liquor shelf. A signed Andre Reed jersey hung in a frame by the pool table toward the side door. Scarface ran on the only television that was on.

"Yeah, I tried. I'm happy with it." He drained his beer and by the time he set it on the bar, Rhonda had a fresh one sweating on a new napkin.

Our weekends of debauchery didn't stop with him. This was his life and the drinking had him in a death lock.

"When you going back to work?"

"Tomorrow." He was staring at his beer, rolling up the corners of the napkin in tight little rolls. His skin was starting to yellow.

"This place looks way better that Carlyle's ever did. You did a good job."

"Thanks brother."

"Yeah man."

There was a nice steady stream of customers. He really turned the place upside down and finally had something he was proud of. But all he cared about now was "The Irish Duo Pub and Grill" and the barmaid feeding his addiction. The family was starting to get getting the picture.

"We don't have a plan yet. We're just seeing where it goes tonight." He was starting to slur his words. That was code for *I'm going to drink until closing, then finish off a case when I get home, and top off the night with an argument with Rhonda.*

"Well I have school in the morning so I can only stay for a few."

Someone walked through the door and sat next to me; a familiar face, with familiar dirty blonde hair. She still has the round hips I love.

"Howdy stranger." Joey said.

"Well look who just breezed in the door." I said. My barstool creaked in her direction. Life clearly slapped the shit out of Joey so I was glad to see it considering how we had left things.

"How have you been?" Her pupils were dilated. She was clearly happy to see me.

"You know ups and downs." I answered. "Can I buy you a beer?"

"Yeah." I waved down to Rhonda and Joey ordered a Coors Light. *Figures.* Her fake tan stopped at her hairline and accentuated the crow's feet around her eyes. Her short halter top she was wearing did not conceal the muffin top that spilled over her jeans and I do not think she cared. Her massive breasts looked like soft water balloons that would fall to her belly button if she took her bra off. She looked like trash and it was a shame.

We decided to play a few games of pool. I really wasn't paying any attention. Every time she leaned on the table to take a shot, her watery belly hung like a cow's utter.

"You want to come back to my place? I have beer there. I also have a little stash of booger sugar if you're interested." She offered.

"Sure. Give me your address and I'll meet you there." I agreed. *Why am I doing this????*

I drove out to Donald Junction to a trailer she lived in just on the edge of town. *Of course she lived in one.* On the drive there I thought of several scenarios to get her naked and fuck her fat ass. It was general principle, *GP's man*, as Junior would say. I knew she was seriously interested in me and I had demons to exorcise. Karma's a bitch. I walked in and clothing and wrappers were everywhere. The pictures on the mantle showed three children that all looked like Joey in a different way. The boy in one of the frames resembled the baby I once knew. Her middle child, a girl, had curly hair just like Joey's but it was red, and a younger daughter that had her icy blue eyes. I immediately felt sorry for them because of who their mother was. They were great looking kids, but they lived in garbage.

"Kids are with their Dads."

"Plural?"

"Yeah, I made more than a few mistakes, all different Dads." We sat on the couch and she leaned in. "I'm sorry for what I did to you."

"It's all good, water under the bridge." I lied. "It's fine."

She reached under the couch cushion and came out with an amount of coke just under the size of a golf ball and started chopping it on the coffee table that showed years of razor blade scars. *Explains how she got so weathered.* She licked the blade clean, rolled a dollar and passed it to me. *Why am I here? Did she screw me up that bad that I have to give her an anger bang? She's disgusting. FUCK!*

"You want any cash for this?" I asked.

"Just fuck me and we're even."

Good god man! What a shame. I thought.

She told me she wanted to move in with me. My plan had worked. By the time I left her early the next morning, she realized what that night was all about.

Joey LaBeauf now lives in Buffalo. She had married and divorced four times. Her drug habits haven't changed, and currently lives on welfare.

3

I woke up late that afternoon sick to my stomach. I couldn't believe I did that. I felt so dirty and disgusting that I couldn't even look at myself in the mirror. It was that afternoon I realized I stayed at the party too long. I was twenty-seven. Guys like Jimi Hendrix and Kurt Cobain had lived and died by twenty-seven. I hadn't done shit. Just like Dad said. I had never even left the state of New York except for a few trips over the border to the strip joints in Canada. *The Canadian Ballet.* I had about a semester and a half of college classes to my credit and by the rate I was going I would earn my Associates just under the age of fifty. I had friends from high school that were already making fifty, sixty grand a year and I'm scraping by with any job I could find.

I decided Andy Dufresne was right. 'Get busy livin, or get busy dyin.' So I chose livin.

I got a job on the local sort at UPS. Pam of course pulled some strings with a few contacts she knew within The Big Brown Machine. It was a physically HARD job but I loved it and the prospect of a career delivering packages for a union wage was comforting.

Junior was in a bad state. He stopped taking care of himself. This was a guy built like a house and now the alcohol was eating his muscle mass. His skin looked yellow or grey depending on how the sunlight hit him. The police force sent him to rehab, a perk within their collective bargaining agreement. I heard around the campfire his business partner told Junior he couldn't come by the bar until he was clean. So after a few weeks he signed himself out and went back to work, the first of many trips.

"How was the stint in rehab? I thought you had to stay for thirty days like in the movies." I said. I walked through the back door of Dad's house to the smoking room, which was filled with a fog of second hand thick as maple syrup.

"No. You can stay that long but I don't need it. You can check out anytime you want. So I did."

"Really?" I asked as I stared at the beer in front of him.

"Yeah, I think I'm a functioning alcoholic."

"No Junior, you're not. You miss a lot of work, that's not normal." Sheri, who also sat in front of a beer, was genuinely concerned.

"He's not gonna listen," Dad piped in, "silly bastard."

Junior laughed at that. "Well maybe you're right." He said gulping down the rest of his beer.

"I'm just glad to see ya. Are you back running The Duo?" I asked.

"I hope so. Mesha is suing me for back child support, so I need all the money I can get right now. I might sign over the bar to my partner until this blows over. She's starting to piss me off."

"Well stay at work! You won't have to worry about it then." Dad said throwing his hands up. "She's not doin anything illegal. You're the bonehead here." He points to his ear. "Lotsa bone lotsa cartilage." He sucked the last of his cigarette to the filter and crushed the butt in the ashtray in front of him.

Junior stood quietly with his beer. "Righteous Dad sittin over there…" He finally said.

That was my cue. I'm not one for confrontations. "I gotta run, work in the morning. I'll see everyone later." I wasn't sticking around to see what was brewing. But Junior was Dad's favorite. He could do no wrong. I have accepted the role of the black sheep. I'm the kid who cannot hold a job for more than a year and is always broke; Junior, the business owner and cop, GOLDEN BOY.

I got home around nine, and it was perfect timing. Pam's kids were in bed. I had bought a twelve pack on the way home and was loading them in the fridge when Pam walked in the kitchen.

"Hey." She was fresh out of the shower, with wet hair, wearing flannel pajamas.

"Hey. I'm gonna hang out on the deck, ok?" *Late night pity fest, here I come.*

"Yeah," She permitted, "I'm tired. Good night, don't stay up too late."

"Ok. Good night."

I grab a beer and walked out to the deck. It's was a clear, lukewarm, summer night. I set my phone on the railing and it immediately lit up in the dark like some magic trick. Jerald's number was displayed on the screen.

"Hey man."

"Hey Unc."

"You ok? Angelina's second heart surgery is tomorrow, right?" When Angelina was born, she would fall asleep unexpectedly at various times throughout the day. They thought she had narcolepsy.

"Yeah, just nervous, ya know?"

"No, I don't know. I'm sorry you have to do this." I cradled my phone between my ear and shoulder while I twisted the cap off my beer bottle.

"It's ok."

"Besides, she's a fighter like us Benton's. She's gonna be golden, you watch."

"Yeah... hey, you remember when we used to get a few deuce-deuces and mob around like we owned the city?"

"Yeah, we'll do it again. After Angelina gets better and you have less on your mind."

"Yeah, ok, that would be cool." The phone fell silent.

"She has one more after this right?"

"Two years. They want to do it before she turns five. She did so well with the first one and they think this one is gonna go good too, so the Doc thinks instead of doing the third one next year, they can wait to do it in two years."

"See? That's good news right? That's 2008. She's awesome. You have nothing to worry about."

"It just sucks she's not gonna live long, ya know?"

"Hey, whoa... the advances in modern medicine these days, when she's forty we'll have medicine and procedures that would make her brand new. Don't worry. She's gonna bury YOU. I guarantee it."

"Yeah, I guess... God, an abnormal heart deformity... Why her, what did she do??"

"I really wish I had an answer for you." More than anything I wish I had an answer to his question.

"Anyway, I gotta run, I'll talk to you later."

"Ok brother," The phone was silent but he was still on the other end of the line, "and Jerald?"

"Yeah Unc?"

"Take a breath. You have nothing to worry about."

4

Dad was sitting on the back steps putting his sneakers on when I walked through the back door.

"Did I catch you at a bad time?" He had a plastic mug next to him on the steps full of water, his traveling beverage.

"Actually, no, let's go for a ride."

"Where?"

"To Junior's, we're taking him to rehab." Dad said as he rose from the steps with a grunt.

"Is he that bad?"

"I'm afraid so. Rhonda's gonna kick him out if he doesn't go."

"Alright, I'll go with you." I offered.

We went out the door toward the garage. Dad's head hung low and eyed the stones in the driveway as he walked. "I don't understand this crazy bastard. He's a COP! I taught him better than this."

"I have no idea." I said. "I can't tell you what's going on in his brain."

"Your sister's are turning their back on him. Mesha wants to throw his sorry ass in jail. She called me last week; he owes six thousand dollars in back child support."

"Jesus." I said. "What's he gonna do?"

"Dunno, not my problem anymore."

We arrived at his apartment on Buffalo Avenue, and entered without knocking. The window in the front door was smashed out and covered with duct tape where he had broken in after Rhonda had locked him out. There was a pile of Budweiser bottles by the front door that stunk of stale beer. The kitchen sink was overflowing with dirty dishes that looked weeks old. A good dozen cigarettes floated in the sink water, some looked like they only had a drag or two pulled off of them. A half dozen more empty beer bottles askew on the counter by the sink accompanied more dirty dishes. Stacked on the breakfast bar were eight cases of empties. Judging by those cases he started to buy cheaper beer like Busch, Keystone, and Natural Ice.

There were cigarette burns and stains all over his living room rug. The apartment smelled of food that was just starting to go bad, probably from the piles of dishes in the sink. Junior was laying back on his recliner watching ESPN. He looked up at us and back to the television.

"We're takin you to rehab." Dad said.

"Ok." Junior answered without hesitation.

"Rhonda can't take it anymore."

Junior rolled his eyes at that. He waved a hand at us. It was slow and ungraceful. He looks at Dad and says, "Whool care about her." He slurred.

"You have nowhere to go." Dad said. "You're not comin back with me. I'm not puttin up with yer shit."

Junior stared at Stewart Scott on the TV screen.

"We're all worried about you." I piped in. "I'm afraid your heart is gonna give out being as bad off as you are."

He looked at me and sighed. He was thinking about it. He wasn't too smashed yet. It was only 9:30 in the morning, by noon it would be a different story. Around that time, he would pass out and sleep to about five or six in the afternoon, then start another shift of slamming beers or whatever seven dollar bottle of vodka he had stashed away. That was his routine.

"Rhonda says she hasn't been here in a week, stayin at her friends? She said she ain't comin back until you're gone. So what's it gonna be?" Dad asked.

Junior looked at the TV. He lets out a huge defeated sigh and says, "Ok, we go tomorrow."

"Are you sure?" Doubt saturated Dad's voice.

"Yeah. I gotta go….I gotta go…." Junior conceded. He started to squirm in his chair.

"I'm beatin the door down if ya don't let me in."

"I'm goin. Morrow…. I'll be reh--…." He started hiccupping. He was trying to keep his mouth closed and holding them in so they sounded like little beeps. He had a beer next to him getting warm. He didn't touch it the entire time we were there.

"I'll be back at seven tomorrow morning. Be ready." Dad said shaking his finger at Junior. Junior was jumping in the chair with a slow rhythm of hiccups. He burped and it sounded like a muffled machine gun.

"Ok?" Dad asked.

"Ok." Junior answered. Dad started for the door.

"I love you. We just want you to get better." I said.

"I love y---." Junior said, before a hiccup cut it short.

"See you tomorrow." Dad said. I followed him to his truck. We sat in the parking lot for a while in silence.

"You think he will go tomorrow morning?" I asked.

"He better, he has no choice."

"I don't know. You want me to come with you?"

"No. It should be alright. I'll take him."

"Where, to the V.A. in Buffalo?"

"Yeah, he has no choice." Dad stared through the windshield. "He has no choice."

5

I thought we were doing some good every time we took him to rehab. But we weren't. When you're an addict, you have to want to help yourself. You can't force an addict. It's up to them. It's their decision to get sober. It is ALWAYS their decision to get sober. It is ONLY their decision to get sober.

Junior called me the Saturday before Mother's Day.

"Hey." I answered.

"Hey. I think we should she our Mudthers on Mudthers Day." He slurred.

"Ok. We should do that. I like that idea."

"So we're goner do that then? Me an you goner she our Mudthers."

"What time?"

Silence. He talked so slow when he was drunk.

"How 'bout noon."

"Ok. I'll call you at noon."

"K, we... will go she our Mudthers. You... an... me." He sloshed.

It was painful to listen to. "Ok, Junior."

"She our Mudthers."

How many times are you gonna say it. WAKE UP, Junior!! "Ok, I'll call you."

"K."

I picked him up the next day and we made the forty minute drive to Gate of Heaven Cemetery in nearby Lewiston. He stunk of stale beer. The aroma was so strong I could have caught a buzz from being around him. We drove through the large light colored gate made of wrought iron, and cast in the shape of the Pearly Gates. Right in front, there are a row of beautiful mausoleums. The north wall had little spots where sad souls lay their children to rest. Along the south wall were the cremated remains of my sibling's mother.

"Hey Ma." Junior said. We walked over to his mother's little maker in the ground. On the way, he kicked a vase of flowers over that was set at the plot next to us and he haphazardly set it back up, leaving the small pile of soil that poured out of it. He stood there in silence with tears in his eyes. I stood behind him and let him have his moment. He held that puppy in like a champ. We Benton boys do not cry in public. That's an unwritten law and that is final. After a few moments, he choked in a breath of air and smoothed out the front of his coat.

"Less go see Sandy." He said turning in my direction.

"Ok." We turned and started walking toward my mother's plot. Junior pulled out a whiskey flask from his jacket and took a swig. Beer foam spilled out of the top and ran onto his fingers. We walked the two hundred yards straight down the path past the other mausoleums and made a right at the fork in the road. Down about forty yards from the fork, six rows in was my mother's plot, complete with an empty spot to the left where Dad reserved what he liked to call his *eternal couch*. To the right is Grandpa Alvin, and Grandma Edna. Some years back a couple snuck in between the Benton plots, and we made jokes about the couple "moving into the Benton neighborhood." Morbid jokers we Benton's are. It comes with the territory when you see a lot of death.

My mother's tombstone is a large circular job that stood a good four feet in diameter, maybe even four and a half. My uncle planted shrubberies around both stones and they had gotten overgrown blocking Dad's half of the stone. It read,

SANDREA L.
1948-1983

It was 1995 at Cora's burial the last time I stood there in the grass at the foot of the plot. I know my mother isn't there. Why visit? Why stand there and say something profound? She isn't going to hear it. She doesn't exist anymore. She was a blip in the fabric of cosmic space-time. We all are in the grand scheme of things. All I know is I was cheated out of my mother in this life and there was nothing I can do about it to change it. I have to like it or lump it. That's the bottom line.

"Hey Papa!" Junior said. He leaned in and kissed Grandpa's stone. At that moment I wished I knew where my other Grandpa was buried, my best friend who I watched Yankees games with. He was in the other direction. East of Niagara Falls in North Tonawanda where he rested with his masonic brothers.

"Ok. I'm cool." I said to Junior.

"Wanna see Cora?" He asked taking another swig from his flask.

"Sure, while we're here."

"Yeah, my is well." He slurred. He was sobering. His speech was coming back slowly. "While we're here."

We knew where she was, to the left and kitty-corner from my mother. Her stone was a small simple marker that read,

Coralline Benton
1948-1995

Junior immediately walked up to it, bent down and slapped his middle finger against her name. "Fuck you bidtch." He stammered. "Fuck you... feck you." Every word he banged his fist with his middle finger extended to emphasize his feelings. I sat back and watched the play unfold.

She's not here to hear that dude. I thought. *If it makes you feel better. You look like a retard, but whatever.*

No matter how I felt at that moment, it meant shit. She won. She doesn't ever have to hear what I had on my chest. *You won, Cora.* I thought. *But you know what? I forgive you. You didn't know any better, you did the best you could. Shit happens. I'm going to try to not let it bother me anymore. I forgive you.*

Cora married a man with four kids and was left to raise them herself while he slept his life away on the couch still grieving the loss of the love of his life. She did the best she could. They were never a physical, loving couple. I never saw them display affection toward each other. Maybe she was deprived of affection from my dad and took it out on me. I stood on her grave that afternoon and decided to forgive her. I felt better immediately.

"Shorty jess wanned a mudther. He gah you. Whatta joke." He said. I hoped he felt better after getting that off his chest. "Fucker."

"Alright, I'm getting depressed. Let's boogaloo brother." I said. He drained his flask and but it back in his jacket. He screwed a Marlboro in his teeth and started fumbling around for his lighter.

"Aight." He answered. He turned and faced Cora's marker, snatched his cigarette out of his mouth and said clear as day, "And see ya later cunt!"

6

"Fuck." I said under my breath. I parked my truck in the driveway and through the front bay window curtains, I could see Pam's kids lounging on the couch in the living room. They were watching *"Adult Swim,"* which was a cool show. But I would much rather shoot myself in the face that walk through the front door. I can't stand this place anymore. I used to like this cozy little ranch Pam owned out right. It had a quaint charm. I don't even know why I am still here. I can't stand her lazy kids. She lets them have the run of the joint. Earlier that afternoon I checked the TV listing and noted "A Few Good Men" was to come on at nine, and I planned on watching it. I just wanted to come home, kick up my feet, suck on a beer bottle or two, watch the movie, and go to bed. Is that so much to ask? I work twelve hours a day that sandwiched a two hour workout at the gym. I just wanted a little peace when I got home. Somewhere Pam seems to think she accommodates for me but she is sadly mistaken.

I exited my truck and stood in the driveway for a minute. *Just leave. You'll be better off, and your blood pressure will thank you.* I walked to the back deck, set my gym bag down at my feet, and leaned against the railing. *You'll feel better in the morning. She doesn't want any more kids. Your clock is BLARING brother.* I looked up at the moon. It was a clear night. Despite the light pollution, there were a lot of stars. *Even if she caves, reverses her tubal ligation, you want more than one kid. You want your own family.*

I grabbed the knob to the back door. *You've seen so much death. You want to see life for a change. You deserve that at least. You're twenty-nine for fuck sake. Not today I guess.* I opened the door. Pam's kids were on the couch. I walked past to the bedroom where Pam was sitting on the bed with her computer.

"Hey." I said unenthusiastically.

"Hey. How was your day?" She asked still staring at her computer screen. She was as unenthusiastic as I was.

"Same shit, different day"

"There's dinner in the fridge. I'm going to bed in a second."

"Ok. I'm taking a shower."

I pulled a fresh set of underwear and pajamas from my dresser. Pam went on about what her oldest boy was doing in school and how he was acting out. I just nodded. I tried for seven years to help her with her kids because her ex-husband was never around. So I stepped up. She always gave me shit for trying to help. *You have no idea,* she would say, *you don't have kids, and you can't ground them for that.* They disrespected me at every turn. I just gave up, just like I gave up on our relationship.

After my shower, I grabbed a frosty cold one and headed to the deck. The kids had gone upstairs to their rooms so that made the night better. Out on the deck, I slumped in my favorite Adirondack chair, twisted off the top of my beer and took a long swallow. The window to our bedroom that faced the deck, went dark. I was alone for the night, and it was time for my Jameson stash. I recently built a portable bar setup in the garage, so after I fetched my Jameson and rocks glass I was on my way.

The moon lit up the back yard. The trees at the east end of the lot cast creepy shadows across the grass. It looked so beautiful. I thought of my grandfather. It had been a little over three years since his death, and I still missed him every day. If I became half the man he was I would be a happy man. I thought of my mother, and even if I have a family with kids someday, Grandpa and Mom would never see them. I will never get over that sadness.

Pam's daughter had used my radio. This chick and her fucking 'NSYNC CD's. *Newsflash! They haven't been relevant in ten years!!* I dropped the CD to the wood planks and I fumbled with the radio. *Boneyard baby!* I'm a beer and three neat whiskeys deep when the disc jockey started to play "Still Remains." *Fuck! This song again! They always play this when I'm on the deck and wallowing in my sorrows. It's like they know what I'm doing.* I twisted the volume knob just a little to hear the lyrics. *Miriam baby, you are the one that got away. That's for sure.*

Last I heard she was happy with her sheriff husband and kids. She's probably the woman who baked cupcakes and sends them to school for her kids and their little friends. Pam had looked her up for me a few years back because she knew I wanted to know. I think she wanted me to find out she had moved on so I could. But I couldn't. I thought of the times I rode my bike and later drove by her house and wondered if she was home. I still remembered the way she smelled. Man, what I would give to run my fingers through her hair and kiss her neck line. Just to say hello and see her again. But she moved on. *I have to keep on. This is a week moment brought on by the whiskey. The booze has seeped in and I'm not thinking straight.* I told myself.

"Fuck it, man." I said to the empty back yard. *Fuck her if she can't take a joke right?* I poured two more fingers in my glass for the last drink of the night and I raised it to the moon.

"To my fallen compadres, who aren't here to do this anymore while I cry like a bitch out here..." I thought of David Bones and Finn Markey. I thought of my friends that are moving on and having kids and families. I threw back my whiskey and poured out the last of the bottle for David and Finn.

I'm such a fucking hack.

7

The next morning my brain was trying to shatter my skull from the inside out. I stumbled to the coffee maker and fumbled around with the grinds and a filter until I succeeded to start a batch of Joe. I threw my bathrobe on to go fetch the gazette laying in the front yard. I picked it up and there it was for all to see.

Niagara Falls City Police Officer Resigns.

"Fuck." I said, as I snapped it open. Junior resigned, and it was in the paper for the whole city to see. Our family, his friends, my friends I worked with, everyone. Pam was going to laugh and comment on how much of a lush he was and berate him. *Great, looking forward to that.* "This is perfect, just perfect." I said, and I went back in the house. *This is a new low.* I thought. *Being a cop was his dream. What happened? Stupid question. I know full well what happened. He had a choice and picked the bottle over his life, wife, and now his job.*

Junior liked to disappear when he fell off the wagon. When he spiraled down, he locked up somewhere and drowned his sorrows. I would blow up his cell phone with calls and texts, and would hear nothing in return. Sonya would call me and cry on the phone about how concerned she was for him while she was getting drunk herself, not realizing she also had a problem. It was a vicious circle.

One night on the job, there was a 9-1-1 call about a disturbance at an apartment complex. Junior was the first cop on the scene. When he arrived, a lady sat on the front steps repeating, "The voices told me to do it. The voices told me to do it."

"What?" He asked her.

"The voices told me to do it." She was covered in blood. He asked her where her apartment was, then he ran up the two fights of steps to the landing. He found the door to the apartment ajar. Inside laying on the kitchen floor was a large butcher knife and a little girl of about five or six gasping for breath. There was a hole in her chest the size of a fist from her mother who was told by voices in her head to do it.

He stuck his hand in her chest massaging her heart, trying to start it again. He tried the best he could. By the time paramedics arrived, she was gone. I don't think Junior came back from that.

A little time after his resignation, Junior walked into a 7-11 to get Spaghettios and a twelve pack of Stones for dinner. While he waited to check out, he went headlong into a full blown seizure brought on by the years of alcohol abuse. He was rushed to the hospital and immediately started a harsh withdrawal. He didn't stop drinking at this point.

A few weeks later, a great thing happened. While at home watching ESPN, he took it upon himself to dump his beer down the drain. He then called an ambulance and checked himself into detox. He stayed for little over a month. After he got back, he immediately fell off the wagon. The family wasn't surprised, we knew the routine.

After getting arrested for stealing a seven dollar bottle of vodka at The Junction Liquor Store, he spent a month in county lockup because Dad refused to bail him out. He also had an outstanding warrant for his arrest for failing to pay his child support to Mesha. It was looking grim.

Finally after a few court dates, he was released and back to drinking. But as the fates would have it, he took it upon himself yet again to enter detox while the New England Patriots were in the middle of their historic undefeated NFL Regular Season. He stayed a full three months that time and it stuck. The family had Junior back. No one was more excited that me.

"Have you seen him since he came back Shortaction?" Sonya exclaimed when she called me.

"No, does he look good? You think he has it beat this time?" I wasn't optimistic, but I would never give up on Junior.

"I think so. He's talking about getting back on his feet again and going back to school. He never talked about that."

"I'm gonna stop by Dad's later to see him." I said.

"He looks great. His color is back, he's gaining weight. His personality is back. Junior is BACK!"

I was so excited. I couldn't wait to see him. I ran right over to Dad's house where Junior was staying for a few days.

"Yeah, that's what I'm talking about." I barked as I walked in the door. Junior sat at the breakfast bar with a twenty ounce bottle of Sprite in front of him. "Welcome back, I missed my BROTHER!" I gave him a hug that in reality was a light tackle.

"Howya doin Doctor? I missed *myself*!" Junior answered.

Dad was in the bathroom, Junior and I were alone. "So what did it this time? Why is this time different?" I asked him softly so Dad couldn't hear us. I don't know why I was whispering, Dad couldn't hear a 747 fly through the back yard.

"It's not different. I'm taking it one day at a time. Just one day at a time." He nodded.

"Well that's different. I never heard you say that."

"I did a lot of thinking this last time around, well, I did other times too, but I have a lot of demons." He took a large gulp from his Sprite.

"Don't we all?" I asked.

"I need to take care of things. I have people to apologize too. People hate me."

"They'll come around." I hung an arm around his shoulders. "You need to take care of yourself."

"Thanks for never giving up on me. I will always struggle with this and it means a lot."

"You were my hero growing up," I said, "you still are. I will never give up on you. You're all I got brother."

Junior's face lit up. "I'm back Doctor!"

"That's right bitches!!" We high fived like a couple of school boys.

The toilet flushed and Dad came out of the hallway, still zipping his fly. "So, enough of that." Dad announced. "You two talk to Jerald yet, your cousin?" He pronounced cousin *cousint*. And besides, he was our nephew. "They scheduled Angelina's last surgery in February, so that is comin up. He said she's doin great, everything is copacetic, should be a walk in the park."

"That's good news." Junior said seriously. He drained his Sprite and set the empty by the kitchen sink. Dad went behind him, grabbed the bottle and disappeared into the smoking room where the recycle bin was and returned to the kitchen.

"We're going to have a nice soiree when it's all over." Dad announced.

"Outstanding! Should be fun. A SOBER family get together." I added.

"Yeah." Dad said. "No more surgeries, medicines, hasta luego, muchacho, amigo."

"Dad, you just said, 'see you later friend friend.'" I translated.

It was lost on him.

8

While Eli Manning was showing the Patriots what he thought of their perfect season, Jerald got word that Angelina's last heart surgery was pushed five months to July. It was a bitter sweet time. She still needed the surgery, but she was doing well enough to not need it as originally scheduled.

Pam's friend had a cottage in Pennsylvania and she invited us down to stay for the Fourth of July weekend. Pam thought we needed a vacation. Our relationship at the time was in my opinion, on its last stand. I had started working out again and she caught the workout bug from me so we were spending time in the gym and we had a new common passion to bond over. We thought we'd go down and hang out with her friend (who didn't like me, but I went anyway to be a good sport), burn some steaks on the grill, and knock back a few barley sodas.

Jerald and his wife made the trip to Strong Children's Hospital in Rochester for Angelina's last heart surgery scheduled for July 2nd. Pam and I drove down to Pennsylvania to meet her friend the next night where we unpacked our stuff, set up our sleeping quarters, and fired up the grill. While we had a few beers, Pam's friend told a story about a tornado that had ripped apart the little town of Kane in the late eighties and permanently damaged the railroad tracks in town. We drank, and we talked. Her friend and I were even getting along for a change. At dusk, we watched fireflies and built a roaring fire thanks to Pam and her friend's time in girl scouts.

When we decided to turn in, Pam and I went inside and were looking forward to our night together. I had just finished my shower when my cell rang. Jerald's number was on the screen.

"Hey brother, how's Angelina's recovery?"

"Hey… well, we're having complications." He said.

"Complications… What's going on?"

"The doctor said there is something weird going on. Her immune system isn't doing what it's supposed to."

"Yikes. Where is everybody?"

"Ma is here. She's spreading the word back home."

"She'll be ok man. Remember I told you that?"

"Doctor is giving her 50/50."

"50/50?!? WHAT? It's that serious?" I yelped.

"I guess so." I didn't think he was thinking straight. His voice didn't sound right.

"Dude, we're driving up there in the morning." I offered.

"Ain't you camping in PA?" He asked.

"Don't matter ok? I'll have my phone on all night. Give me a call if you need anything."

"Ok. I'll keep you informed." Jerald said. He broke the connection. I stood with my dead phone to my ear.

Pam stared at me with wide eyes. "What's going on?" She asked.

"I don't know. He doesn't sound right."

"You wanna drive up there? We're only a few hours away… three tops."

"You don't mind?"

"No. Of course not."

"Ok. Something's not right. He's not right. Something is screwy here." I picked up my phone and called Jerald back.

"Hey." He answered on the second ring.

"We're coming up tonight to be with you. I think you need the support. You need me to pick up anything on the way up?"

He missed the last question. "Ok. You know where we are?" He asked.

"Yeah, we'll find you."

"Ok."

Pam and I packed up within twenty minutes and we were on the road to Rochester.

When Angelina was recovering from her second surgery, Pam and I made the trip to Rochester to see Jerald and his wife. We thought we could get them away from the hospital and hang out. Hopefully get their mind off things for a while. They didn't leave her side except to go to dinner. The restaurant was a nice seafood joint I remember. Afterwards we planned on playing Monopoly at the hotel we were staying at. But they decided against it and went back to the hospital with Angelina. They just wanted to stay with her. And I get that now.

Twenty minutes up Route 219, Jerald called me back.

"Hey man, talk to me." I answered.

"We're losing her."

"Jesus." I whispered. "We're driving as fast as we can. We're almost to the border, about an hour and a half, two hours from you. We're coming."

"Ok. I'll keep you informed."

"Ok."

A half our later, he called me back and said something that will be etched in my brain until the day I die.

"What's up brother? Tell me some good news." I said. I was hoping for the best.

"We lost her. She's gone."

"I'm sorry man. We'll be there soon." My head was already swimming. It was like I fell down a rabbit hole.

"Ok." He said. I barely heard him.

Angelina Rose died in the wee hours of July 4, 2008, after contracting a Staph infection that her battered immune system couldn't fight off. She was two months shy of her fifth birthday.

I hung up the phone and cried the entire way to Rochester.

9

The wake was as somber and dark as anyone could imagine. It was a very depressing scene consisting of people standing around quietly sobbing and sniffling. Whispering voices bounced off the walls, like spooky sound effects.

Angelina was by the south wall dressed in a white satin dress. She looked like an angel taking a quick nap during this boring event. It's a heartache you can't quite explain. I cannot begin to imagine what Jerald was feeling. Junior and I were asked to be pall bearers. We told Jerald it would be an honor.

The funeral is an event I wish I could wipe from my memory. It was held at Grace Lutheran Church. A large place we siblings all went to for Catechism. Jerald's wife days away from giving birth to another daughter, was holding everyone together like a saint. They were burying one child, and welcoming another the same week like some sort of sick trade off they were forced into.

The place was eerily quiet. No one could think of anything to say. What do you say to someone who just lost their child? A child that will never grow up, and experience the things in life that makes it worth living. Like a simple kiss on the cheek from the boy down the street. Or having a slumber party with friends, giggling like, well, school girls, and staying up way past bedtime. Or having her heart broken by her first boyfriend and crying to a friend about it, learning that it's better to have loved and lost than to have never loved at all. Or earning the job she always wanted, the job she awoke and stretched to the ceiling with ambition every morning and couldn't wait to get to. Or having a small intimate get together. A get together with good friends, good food, and good conversation. Or meeting the man of her dreams, a man that would worship the ground she walks on, a man that would love her just like Jerald loved her. That was all gone.

Junior and I gathered with two friends of Jerald's by the front of the church, fidgeting like a pair of thieves. A jet black hearse drove up and a slick man in his early forties got out whistling some random tune. He opened the back door and lined up the metal coffin roller. The four of us lifted and started walking through the church. It's a vision that is burned into my memory. It will be one of the memories that will flash through my mind when I die, if that sort of thing in fact actually happens.

I've carried heavy coffins in my day, but this one was light as a feather. It was covered in beautiful pink velour fabric. Her coffin made the whole scene surreal. Inside the church was fuzzy, like this was all a dream. But it was more like a nightmare. Junior and I were the two pall bearers carrying the back. He broke down crying when we started marching through the church, rolling the coffin on the squeaky roller apparatus. People somberly stared as we floated past. More sobbing, more crying.

We stopped and rolled the coffin to the center of the altar. The pastor went through his spiel about God and his plan and blah, blah, blah. I sat there in the first pew and smoke started coming out of my ears. *You know, fuck this guy.* I thought. *Fuck God right in his ass. Who is he to say that Jerald and his wife deserve to go through this because it's a part of a plan and he only gives you what you can handle. Just because he thinks they can handle it, they should have to endure this??? He's a kid with an ant farm. Fuck him, FUCK HIM.*

He doesn't exist. There is too much pain and evil in this world, like this funeral, that happens every day for him just to sit back and let it happen. If I find on the other side that he does exist, on my way to hell he's getting a piece of my mind. *You're a sick prick, you righteous fucker.*

After the sermon, we carried her outside to the hearse again and everyone congregated in the sunshine. Cars drove by, and rubberneckers slowed to steal a peak at this little pink coffin we carried. I got mad all over again. They were the lucky ones today.

When the hearse pulled away it hit me. Something punched me in the stomach and I couldn't breathe. Pam stood by my side, I buried my head in her neck and sobbed.

At UPS later that afternoon, I cried while throwing boxes around in the trailer I was loading. I could have cared less what people were thinking. I did that for a week. People probably thought I was having a nervous breakdown.

10

Things went in a circle for a while. Twelve hours of work sandwiched a workout, then frustration and feelings of alienation would greet me at home. That would be followed by drinking myself to oblivion on the back deck, and I started it all again the next day. While the Yankees were on their way to winning their millionth World Series Championship, and my beloved Orioles finished last in the A.L. East, again, for the eight thousandth consecutive year, Pam woke me up on a beautiful Saturday morning.

"So I talked to a lady at work yesterday." That conversation turned out to be her downfall.

"Yeah?" I asked.

"We were talking about how long we've been engaged."

"Ok..." I started to help her make the bed. I knew there was something on her mind.

"She said it's time you shit or get off the pot, and I agree." I was silent as I smoothed out the fresh sheet we put on our bed. "Are we getting married or what?"

I stopped and I stared back at her. She stood in the sunlight by the window. It made a halo on top of her head that accentuated her wavy brown hair. We had a good run. "Sorry, I cannot marry you." I finally said to her.

"I knew it. I fuckin knew you didn't have it in you." She said, with her face contorted.

"I want kids. I've seen so much death. I have to see some life for a change. I can't give that up. I know I would be a good father." I placed the pillows by the headboard.

"Like you are to my children?" She barked at me condescendingly.

"I'm done." I said throwing my hands up at her. "I'll be back later to pick up my things."

I started walking to the front door. I heard Pam following. I grabbed the door knob, but stopped to look back.

"'I've seen so much death.' WHAA! Cry me a river! You're gonna use that excuse?!?" We stared at each other a few seconds. It seemed like an eternity. "So this is it? This is how ten years ends?" She sobered.

I opened the door and walked out.

Pam still lives in Niagara Falls. Last I heard, she is a champion power lifter, and she currently holds several New York State Records in the Over Forty category. She is happy and is doing what she loves.

11

When I heard of Facebook I thought it was a pretty cool concept. It was nice to see how friends have turned out since high school. Junior, now three years sober, even started one for The Irish Duo Pub and Grill. He posts dinner specials on it all the time. Since getting sober, he put all his efforts into that establishment. He even tore down the dilapidated string of stinky hotel rooms and added a restaurant in its place, with a baseball diamond for "The Irish Duo Galloping Hobo's" bar league softball team. I will never get over him as a recovering alcoholic who runs a bar.

It works for him though. Hey, what do I know?

Miriam friended me on Facebook and periodically I would stalk her page, which consisted of old pictures of all of us back in the day. They brought back memories of things I forgot about long ago, and it made me sad all over again. One time we even chatted on a post and she said we should have a drink some time. Mindless chatter just to be nice.

One day I received a friend request from Sierra. We conversed back and forth long distance, catching ourselves up from about a decade of lost contact. She currently lived out of town and had been married for the last four years. I told her I was starting over after my long relationship. She told me she was currently trying to have children with her husband. It was a nice conversation. I felt jealous that she also was doing great in her life, working at a large University, entering monetary gifts for the Alumni Association. I was angry at where I was in my life and I knew it was my fault.

While everyone was commenting on Facebook on how cool it was that the Academy Awards had more than five Best Picture nominations for the first time since 1943, Sierra posted her brothers obituary. I immediately commented on her status expressing my heart felt sorrows because I for one, knew how that felt and if she needed anything, I was available to talk. A few weeks later, she had to put her beloved dog down because he developed cancer. She was having a hard time and I made sure to let her know I was there for her, being old friends and all.

We emailed and messaged one another. We reminisced about days past and life. I was happy because it got her mind off things for a while. We wondered what it all meant. Sierra said she was missing something out of life, I knew that all too well. But mostly these correspondences were of fond memories of days long gone, and how we wished we had them back. It was a good time.

One Saturday night I received a message on Facebook from Sierra. It read,

Hey you! I'll be in Niagara Falls on Monday and Tuesday. What is your schedule like? I thought maybe we can have lunch.

I found that I was excited to get that message. My feelings surprised me. It was an excitement I haven't felt in quite a while. Something stirred in a dark room somewhere in my memories.

I responded with,

I'm pretty busy. I work both days 7-2 at U-Haul and 5-9 at UPS. Where are you going to be staying?

I checked for a response the next day and Monday morning before I went to work. No replies.

It was like any other day. The parking lot of U-Haul was bare except the moving vans that snaked by the door like a conga line. I turned my key in the lock of the side door and pulled the handle. A slow steady song of dings told me to disarm the security system. My personal code was 1983, a number connected to the year I will never forget. The word

DISARMED flashed on the glowing green bar on the system key pad by the door. I weaved through the hitch bay that was littered with various tools and wire clippings to the front counter. I cranked up the computer, which was the latest and greatest about ten years ago, and ran the opening reports. It was seven o'clock. Usually I surfed the web until Barry, the store manager, arrived around eight.

At 8:35, Barry's 2000 Dodge Magnum screamed through the parking lot and parked by the back door. He was a little tardy, but it was always ok with me because he would let me go on Timmy's runs on company time.

He strolled in nonchalantly through the lobby door. He always had a shit-eating grin on his face. "What's up?"

"Hey man."

"Anything exciting this morning?" He leaned against the counter and snapped the switch on his ancient computer.

"About as exciting as watching paint dry."

He stretched is arms to the ceiling and his shoulder and elbow joints made audible pops; he followed it up by rolling his head to crack his neck.

"Man, I'm tired." He confessed.

"You want anything from Timmy's?"

"I dunno know man." He exhaled and rubbed his beer gut. "I have to cut down a little on the carbs."

"Yikes! Good luck with that brother... Coffee?"

"Yeah, get me my usual." His usual was an extra-large triple-triple, meaning three creams and three sugars. He started digging in his pocket.

"Nah, I got this." I offered.

"Really?"

"Yeah. A dollar eighty's not gonna break me. Besides, you bought the last time."

"Thanks. I'll getcha next time."

"Cool. Buffalo dropped the ten-footer they're giving us." I pointed to the small U-Haul parked out front. He turned and gazed out the window to the parking lot.

"Is it clean? They like to transfer complete shit to us." He twisted the soul patch under his lip with his thumb and index finger.

"Fuck no. It's full of mud." I reported.

"I'm charging them bastards."

"Good, them FINKS," my stomach growled, "I'll be right back."

I snagged my keys from the hook mounted under the counter and headed out to Tim Horton's on the corner of Niagara Falls Boulevard just three blocks up. The drive-thru was usually packed this time of the morning, but when I turned in the parking lot it was clear as a bell. I ordered Barry's triple-triple, and my usual; a medium coffee, with one creamer and no sugar, and a sausage, egg, lettuce, and tomato breakfast sandwich on a twelve grain bagel. It's perfect for workout days and especially tasted fabulous on shitty Monday mornings. On the short drive back to work, I noticed the sun was trying to poke through a thin wisp of clouds in the warm air. I turned into U-Haul's parking lot and a lady in a Kia Sportage was creeping through.

"What the fuck is this chick doing??" I asked my dashboard. She crept a few more feet, turned, and parked in front. I revved past her car acting like a typical road raged New Yorker and parked back in the same space I did earlier that morning. I walked through the back door and weaved through the hitch bay now swept and tools returned to their homes. Barry was on the internet checking his profile on some off the wall social network for vampires. I set his vat of coffee by his arm.

"Thanks man, a girl was here looking for you." He said.

"Pam?" I asked. Three years of working with me at U-Haul, he knew exactly who Pam was. I was still bracing for her to show her face one of these days.

"No, some new girl. I never saw her before."

"Really?"

"Yeah..." He nodded. "Great looking..." He described. "Exotic."

"Huh." I shrugged. "The plot thickens."

I unwrapped my sandwich and took a sip of my coffee. It was perfect. I had the latest edition of Muscle Mag stashed under the counter that I liked to read when the store was empty. I leafed through it as I chewed my sandwich. *Add ten pounds to your bench press in a week*! It exclaimed.

A customer opened the front door. There was a distinct two-tone chime that echoed through the store. I had come to hate that chime. That time was no different. When I heard it, I looked up from my magazine.

12

She strolled up the aisle with a cool seduction. She wore faded jeans and a heavy white sweater that fit her like magic despite it not matching the weather outside. Large dark lensed sunglasses that looked like something Bono would wear concealed her eyes. Her hair was dark, curly, and looked like a dream. I stared at her until she cocked her head to the left, and removed her shades.

"Oh my god," I exclaimed, "Oh my God!"

"Hey!" She giggled as she continued toward me. "Oh my God," I repeated, "Oh my God. How have you been?!?"

I hugged her, lifting her off the ground. I could smell a floral Herbal Essence in her hair, still soft and thick as I remembered it. "I'm good, how have you been?" She asked.

Barry was watching this all unfold. "Hey brother, can I have a second outside with her? I haven't seen this woman in like, twelve years." I asked.

"Yeah, it's ok. Go." Barry approved.

"I can't believe you're standing here."

"Hug me again." She asked. Again, I lifted her off the ground and buried my face in her hair. It smelled heavenly. She gave out a soft groan in my ear.

We headed for the door. Sierra walked ahead me; her jeans looked fantastic on her behind, nice and compact. "Stop staring at my ass, Shorty." She said, like she had eyes in the back of her head.

I busted out laughing. "All these years you still got my number."

"Some things never change." She looked over her shoulder and smiled.

I walked her to the Kia Sportage, and I put the two together. "I was swearing at you five minutes ago for creeping in the parking lot like a tourist."

"My aunt's car. She's letting me borrow it while I'm in town." She leaned against the passenger door. She crossed her arms in front of her breasts, I noticed her wedding ring. It was a symmetrical diamond cut, on a gold band, with a wedding band on the outside, the wrong order.

"So I'm sorry about your dog. That must have sucked. You had a pretty rough go the last few months."

"Yeah, he was such a sweet dog. You would have loved him." She turned her gaze toward the road. "You were the only one of my friends who was there for me."

"Hey, I know how it feels losing someone close like that. We don't have the time to get into that right now." She looked back at me. Her hair blew away from her face. It was smooth and still pretty as I remembered. "So I want to meet the lucky bastard you're married to."

"Have you talked to Amanda lately?" She asked.

"No. Last we talked was five years ago. She stopped by for a visit, and then promptly moved to North Carolina."

"I know. She lives in Raleigh, about fifty miles away from me. Cut me off three years ago."

I shuffled my feet on the pavement. "That chick is weird. Fuck her if she can't take a joke." Sierra laughed. She still had her amazing laugh too. "When you were on Facebook, I said I wanted to meet the lucky bastard you married. Now I said it again. Why are avoiding the question? Am I being too nosy? I'm sorry."

"He's not with me."

"Oh."

"Oh, well that isn't going so well either."

"Yikes." I said.

"Yeah, I'm in the process of leaving."

"I'm sorry to hear that."

"Oh, it's ok. I left back in October, but I went back because we decided to try to make it work. But it's not working."

I shook my head. "Ouch. That's tough."

"Well, it is what it is." She shrugged.

"So how long are you in town?" I asked, breaking up the depression.

"Just a few days until Wednesday… My Mom's in the hospital. She was up here visiting a friend and she started having chest pains. So here I am."

"I hope your Mom is ok." I couldn't take my eyes off her. "I can't believe you're here."

"You already said that." She smirked at me, the same sly smirk she had back in high school. It still drove me crazy. "You want to go to lunch with me or not?"

"Sure. I get off at two. Let's exchange cell numbers so I can text you when I'm done."

"Ok." She enters my number in her phone. It was the newest iPhone.

"Alright then, it's a date. Well sort of." I said.

"I'm gonna go." She said.

She stretched her hands up to my neck and came in for another hug. She looked up at me and I froze. Life was good to her. She still had a smooth baby face and her olive skin accentuated her hazel eyes. Subconsciously, I just went for it and kissed her. We had kissed one time in high school playing spin the bottle, and we were not in rhythm. This time we were, and she kissed back like she really wanted it. I will never forget it. We broke and she looked up at me like this was the most natural thing she has ever done. I buried my hand in her hair just above the back of her neck and kissed her again. It was like we had been doing this for years.

She got in her car, she wiggled her fingers when she waved, and drove out of the parking lot. I went back in the store and Barry was sipping his coffee and perusing the internet. He was oblivious to what just happened outside.

"I haven't seen her in YEARS, man."

"She's cute." He said.

"Yeah... dark and exotic, just the way I like them." I said. My cell phone vibrated with an incoming text.

SIERRA: Did that just happen?

I stared at it for a while. It did. I couldn't believe it, but it happened. So I text back,

ME: Yeah. What was that all about?

A few moments later,

SIERRA: I thought it was a dream.

ME: No. It definitely happened.

SIERRA: See ya after work.

When two o'clock rolled around I found her waiting in the parking lot, parked by my truck.

"Your vehicle or mine?" She asked.

"We can take my truck."

She killed the Kia's engine and walked around to the passenger side of my Dodge. It was too high for her. She had to jump into the seat.

"Need a booster seat?" I grinned.

"Shut up." She laughed. "I can't help that your truck is too big."

"Feels just right to me."

She exhaled and settled into the seat. "So, where do you want to eat?"

"I'm not all that hungry." I said.

"Me either."

"Let's go for a ride. We have some catching up to do." I turned down the boulevard. "How is it living in North Carolina? Amanda told me some time back you moved there, like, ten years ago."

"It's beautiful. I can't remember the last time I seen snow. I live in Mebane. It's a small town about thirty miles west of Durham."

"I have a cousin that lives in Charlotte." I made a right down Forester Street in Donald Junction. The clouds thickened and struggled with the sun all morning and the day shaped out to be cool and overcast.

"Can you turn the heat on? I'm freezing." She put an ice cold hand on my cheek.

"Wow, you're not kidding." I turned the dial from blue to red and clicked it to the second notch.

"I finally convinced my family to move down in 2006. They love it. They will never move back."

"I wish I could get out of here. Nothing's left but my ghosts."

I pulled in to the parking lot of the pizza parlor on the corner of Forester Street. The sweet smell of pizza sauce and garlic was blowing through the dashboard vents.

"Are you sure you're not hungry? Don't let me stop you."

"Yeah, I'm fine."

"I don't miss this weather." She rubbed her hands on her thighs. The last twelve years have been very good to her.

"Why did Amanda cut you off?"

Sierra shook her head. "I have no idea. If I had to guess, it probably has something to do with her husband."

"Makes sense." I agreed.

"When she moved down there to be with that guy, we immediately got back in touch. We hung out all the time. It was great, I had my best friend back."

"Did you ever meet the guy?"

She rubbed her hands together and tucked them between the seat and her legs. "Yeah, he's big and fat, and a total wackadoo. We went to dinner with our husbands one time, and the entire meal he was slamming beer and flirting with the waitress right in front of her. He's a total ass. That's my impression of the guy."

"You're sitting on your hands. You need more heat?"

"No this is perfect." Her neck and face was the only skin visible. It was tan and looked quite dark against the contrast of her white sweater. "Anyway, she's happy. He's some big shot engineer so she married for money. They live in this gargantuan house. There's no way she married him because he's a great guy."

"Hey, if that's the life she wants. I don't care about me. But you two were close. It's a shame she can't grow up."

"Whatever."

"That's right." I said. "Fuck her if she can't take a joke."

Sierra giggled. "So what was that about this morning?"

I turned the heat down to the lowest setting. "You tell me. You were the one looking up at me waiting for me to kiss you."

"What?!?" She bounced and turned toward me in her seat. "I'm short. I was just looking up!"

"Likely excuse. You kissed back."

She smirked at me. That smirk was beginning to turn into my kryptonite. "Why didn't we date back in high school?"

"You hated me remember? I treated your best friend like shit."

"You were supposed to work your way around the circle. That's what you do in high school. You dated Miriam, then got hung up on Amanda."

"We wouldn't have lasted in high school. You were prude as hell. You were no good to me. I was a complete asshole. You would hate me today if we dated back then."

I placed my hand on her knee. Her jeans were warm. "I guess I lost my chance. My loss." She looked into my eyes and smiled. She grabbed my hand. "You're beautiful. Life has been good to you."

"You too." She said.

I ran my hand up to her hip. She leaned in and we kissed. We fit together, perfect, like an artist and his muse. I would have killed for her. All of a sudden, I couldn't take my hands off of her.

"Wow, we got to go someplace where we can be more private." I finally said. My penis was so hard, I could have broken concrete with it. "Is there a place we can go where you're staying?"

"We can't."

"Why?"

"I'm gonna do this right. I'm not going to cheat. We will have our time. Trust me."

"You're right. I'm not thinking straight." I panted. My logic was in my pants.

"Some things never change." Sierra smirked.

She was busy on Tuesday. Her mother turned out fine, and was back on her feet. I wanted to see her again before she went home, but it wasn't meant to be. I thought I would never see her again.

13

We started texting back and forth after her visit. Innocent stuff like, "How's your day going?" Nice conversations, usually consisting of every day mundane things.

A week later, I was in the hitch bay at U-Haul. I was running wire underneath a Ford F-150 when Sierra's number lit up my phone screen.

"Hey Sweetie, how are you?"

"I did it."

"You did what?" I was laying on a creeper snipping off excess zip tie ends. We used them to hide trailer plug wiring along brake fluid lines.

"I left."

"What?" I watched Barry's feet walk past my vision.

"Yeah, I'm staying at my Mom's for now. I already shopped apartments and I found a studio here in town."

"Wow, you have been busy."

"I miss you." She said.

"I miss you too. It was a nice visit."

"Why don't you come down here to visit? I move into my new apartment May 15th. Come down for your birthday. What do you think?"

"Well, I think I have a few vacation days saved. I can stay for extended weekend. Leave here on a Friday, stay until maybe Tuesday."

"Perfect. Oh and I almost forgot, this apartment complex has a pool."

"Oh, that could be dangerous." I thought of Sierra in a bathing suit. I would lose my mind.

"So is it a plan?"

A proper vacation. It sounded like a great idea. I stared at the Ford's exhaust pipe that was inches from my face. "Yeah, I think it's a plan."

"Great! I'll show you around. You're not gonna want to leave."

You're 100% right on with that one baby. Niagara Falls is dead and I'm slowly dying with it. "Probably. I'll start setting it up on my end."

"Ok."

"I…"

"What was that?"

"Never mind, I'll talk to you later." I broke connection. *Did I almost tell her that I loved her? Probably habit. Ten years of lip service toward Pam.*

I set up the trip to leave on Saturday, May 29th and stay until June 1st. The morning before the trip I received a package at U-Haul from Sierra with four numbered gifts inside and instructions to open them in order. They were a Muscle Mag magazine, a memoir written by a music critic, an iTunes gift card, and a key to her apartment. The key was one of the best gifts I had ever received.

On Facebook that night, I had noticed my page still said "In a Relationship." So I turned that off. An hour later almost on the tick I get a private notification from Miriam that reads,

How about a drink?

It's funny. She never said more than three words to me on that site. I knew this could be dangerous. Miriam and Sierra were never the best of friends. In high school Sierra would tell Miriam about a guy she liked and then Miriam would immediately ask them out. High school drama at its best.

It was eight o'clock. I was already in for the night. But something burned in me. I replied,

Irish Duo? 10pm?

About ten minutes later,

Sounds good.

I gotta see her. All this history, I gotta see her.

14

I arrived about ten minutes late. As I was backing into a parking spot, I noticed a lady standing by the front door. I killed the engine and looked in my rearview mirror. The lady looked familiar but it can't be. It just can't be.

I exited the truck and made my way to the door. I was a well-oiled machine. I was in the best shape of my life thanks to my rigorous gym schedule. I had the body that rivaled Matthew McConaughey. I knew that when I showed up in faded blue jeans, a white fitted dress shirt with rolled sleeves that buttoned, and dress shoes, I came to impress.

Miriam on the other hand, was wearing jeans and a red blouse. A belly roll was bulging the blouse just enough for me to notice. Her beautiful curly hair was gone and a shoulder length mousy brown mane replaced it. She had braces some years back to straighten her teeth which now looked weird to me and they had yellowed from smoking.

"Hi! How have you been?" She greeted.

"It's been a long time hasn't it?"

We hugged. She smelled like a Marlboro that had been spritzed with Obsession for Women. "Almost twenty years." She said nodding like a Bobblehead. "We shouldn't wait this long again to see each other."

"I hear you." I opened the door for her and we walked inside. Junior was not there. He usually leaves for the night around seven. If he was, he would have taken care of me and made me look like a big deal. I didn't need it that night. "So what are you drinking stranger?" I asked. Two open stools were at the corner by the front door.

"Coors Light." She answered. *Of course, you want Coors Light, a drinker's beer.*

I ordered her Coors and a Guinness for me. A cool cat named Nate Clingersmith was the hipster behind the bar who played bass in the band that plays at the Duo two Saturdays a month.

"So what's been going on with you the last twelve years?" I asked.

"You know… regular stuff."

I just launched into it. "So you went off and got married like a thief in the night."

She laughed. "What do you mean?"

"I never got my invite!" I slipped into the bar stool next to her. Her purse was on the bar next to her drink and it smelled just like her; smoke and Obsession.

"I didn't think you would want to go."

"You're right, I wouldn't have."

"Plus it would have been weird for my husband."

"Your daughters are beautiful by the way. They look like you, like the teenage you."

"Thanks." She grabbed my left arm and squeezed my bicep. "Can I tell you how sexy you look right now?"

"Thanks. You too." I lied.

"No way, you're just being nice. I need to lose some weight."

"So, what happened with your husband?" I said changing the subject. "You seemed happy."

She took a large gulp of her Coors Light. "Well he was a great guy in the beginning, but after we had our children he turned abusive."

"That's a shame." More than that, it was quite a shame she let herself go. She was such a beautiful girl. That teenager was long gone. "You were supposed to marry me. But you went off and got married without me."

She sobered. "I had to do it Shorty. I just had to do it for me. I came out of it a wiser person." She looked in my eyes. "Enough about me, what's your story? Ten year relationship, what happened?"

"She wasn't the one. I stayed way too long. I was comfortable."

She nodded. "I know exactly what you mean."

I turned to face her. "There was a reason why we were engaged and I never took the plunge, you know?"

"Waiting for me?" She put a hand on my chest. It was cold and I felt it through my shirt.

"Something like that."

"I can't get over how hot you are."

I smiled at her desperation. "You already said that."

"I'm sorry I led you on all those years back then. I was stoned a lot. I did a lot of stupid things back then."

"You know how many times I walked past your house at night when I couldn't sleep, even when I knew you didn't live there anymore. Or the times I looked up at Orion and wondered if you were doing the same thing?"

"I remember how much I loved that constellation. I haven't done that in years." She gazed down at my thighs. "I'm sorry."

"It's ok, water under the bridge."

She slyly put her hand on my knee. "You know, we can go back to my place. I have beer there. It's Coors Light but good enough to continue this conversation somewhere private."

I looked into her eyes and thought about it for about thirty seconds. *Do it for GP's man,* Junior would say, *GP's. You have demons to exorcise.* That would be the ultimate. The anger bang of all anger bangs. But I was over that now. I'm above it. Besides, the Miriam Roberson I knew is no longer here. Maybe she never was.

"I have a lot to do tomorrow. I need to be up with the birds."

"Ok, maybe you can come camping with me next weekend." She offered as a consolation prize.

"Sounds good." I said, having no intention of going with her.

I left the nine dollars and change on the bar. We stood and headed for the door. We walked to her car in silence and I immediately felt relieved. Years of frustration, anger, and pity left me that night.

"Give me a hug." Now she smelled more like her perfume. I felt her warm belly press against me. "Are you sure you can't come with me for one more?"

She still had those icy blue eyes that used to drive me nuts. But they did nothing for me anymore. "No. I got a million things to do tomorrow morning. Some other time."

"Ok." She got in her car and rolled down the window. "Don't be a stranger. Use that cell number I gave you."

"I will."

"Good seeing you again Shorty." She started the engine.

"You too."

She backed out of her parking spot and headed down the street. I waved at her and watched the red tail lights disappear down the road. It was midnight when I checked the time on the dashboard radio face in my truck. I turned over the starter and "Somewhere Out There" by Our Lady Peace was about half way through on the radio. It was fitting that that song was playing at that moment. It was another song I would hear and contemplate the lyrics wondering what Miriam was doing while I missed her on the deck of pity. I chuckled as I cranked the volume knob.

I drove down Niagara Falls Boulevard that night to Tonawanda and back with the windows down, wind blowing through my hair. I thought of all the times I pined over her and I laughed with the music blasting. The Boneyard was playing great tunes that night and I cruised like I used to. When I got home, I felt like a new man. In a few hours I was going to make the drive to North Carolina and hang out with an old friend, and it excited me the way only a content man could feel.

15

I had to work a few hours at U-Haul the next morning. I quickly knocked out the only hitch installation scheduled, then spent the rest of the time leaning on the counter looking like a statue talking with Barry. At eleven o'clock with a small bag containing a few outfits and a pair of swimming trunks, I headed down the interstate to North Carolina to visit Sierra.

I took the scenic route through the mountain ranges of Pennsylvania and West Virginia. I ran into some thick traffic around Morgantown due to an accident but other than that it was clear sailing. The drive took me just south of nine hours. I was cooking with the gas, pedal to the floor the entire time. When I crossed the Virginia-North Carolina State line, I called her.

"I can't believe you're almost here." She said excitedly.

"Why? What's not to believe?" I asked.

"I just thought you would call and tell me you changed your mind, or just not come."

"Why would I do that? Not on your life."

"I can't wait to see you." She breathed into her phone.

"You're telling me. I love this weather." When I left that morning, it was sixty-eight degrees. In North Carolina, it was ninety, at eight in the evening. "I'll be there in about an hour."

"Don't make me wait too much longer."

"I'm trying."

"Don't kill yourself out there. You're too close now."

"I won't. Trust me."

About forty-five minutes later I saw the sign that read, "Exit 153 Mebane." The excitement in my stomach ratcheted a few notches and I thought I was going to blow my lunch on my steering wheel. After a quick left, and a right a half mile down the road, I turned onto Route 70 which was going to take me the rest of the way to the apartment complex where Sierra lived. I couldn't sit still in my seat. Trying to curb my excitement at this moment, was a lost cause.

I pulled up to the apartment complex and I immediately noticed the pool. It was kidney shaped and even at nine o'clock with moonlight skipping across the water it looked inviting, like it was waiting for me my whole life. The buildings stood in a horse shoe pattern. An even balance of vinyl siding and brick added to its serene atmosphere, and the air was laced with jasmine.

I pulled my truck into the nearest open parking spot and got out to stretch my legs. They gave out from sitting for the last few hours and I stumbled against the side of my truck. Then I heard hard slaps, something was smacking the pavement.

Sierra's flip flops were slapping the pavement as she ran full speed toward me. I had just enough time to look up at her, turn and catch her as she jumped into my arms. We stood in the parking lot of the apartment complex like a beautiful abstract sculpture. The feeling of her legs wrapped around my waist is a feeling I have felt in my dreams before.

"Long drive?" She asked.

"You have no idea." I smiled up at her.

She had a way about her. A subtle seduction and I was putty in her hand. She led me into the apartment. It was cool and it smelled of vanilla. The lights were dim and a candle flickered on a stand in the living area. It was a lovely studio apartment that was as comfortable as warm fleece.

"You want anything to drink? I bought Guinness for you."

"Maybe in a while." I sat down in her chaise lounge. I belonged here.

She came over to me and sat on my lap. "I'm so glad you're here."

"I'm glad too."

We had our time.

16

Sierra and I went to Carolina Beach the next day, and we enjoyed the sun and surf. The weather was absolutely perfect and I couldn't get enough of it. All day we spent soaking up the rays and talking about days past. We had parked her Jeep Cherokee on the beach and when we decided to leave Sierra accidently buried it to the axles. A nice older couple driving a beat up Toyota 4x4 helped us out and we all had a laugh about it. Before our drive back to Mebane we stopped at a seafood restaurant and ate crabs. It was a great day.

We went to a place called Bailey's in Raleigh for my birthday. Sierra never drinks, but she slammed a birthday shot of Jameson with me. She's a real trooper. Afterwards, she took me to the Cheesecake Factory. I'm a *FIEND* for cheesecake. We had carrot cake cheesecake. It was an orgasm on a plate.

We spent some time poolside back at her apartment. I forgot about work, and Niagara Falls the entire time. Tuesday came and I didn't want to go back to Niagara Falls.

"North Carolina agrees with you." Sierra said as she worked on her tan, rubbing Panama Jack on her legs. She was wearing a blue stripped two piece bikini. It drove me crazy all weekend.

"I'm going to call Barry and tell him I can't come back because I have car trouble. I took the whole week off at UPS anyway so I'm covered there. I'm staying the rest of the week. This is too awesome to end now."

"Why don't you just move your ass down here?" Sierra asked. Her hair was wet and she gleamed in the sun from the lotion. The lotion smelled amazing on her.

"I would love too. I love it here. I love..." *You, I almost slipped again!* "I just love it here."

She sat up and took her sunglasses off. I could see the sober look in her eyes. "You know I had to do it."

I was puzzled. "What."

"My husband, I wasn't happy." She started twirling her shades with her index and middle fingers.

"Yeah, you told me."

"That's not it. When my brother passed after his funeral I realized how short life is."

"Huh, I know all too well." I nodded at her.

"I realized I couldn't stay being this unhappy. I always thought you were the one that got away. I always felt that maybe you were waiting for me all these years." She ran her fingers through my hair. It was starting to go thin. But she didn't seem to mind. "I love you."

"I love you too."

I knew the minute she walked into U-Haul a month prior. I can't explain it. It just hits you, no warning when you least expect it. She showed up that fateful day and all the tumblers fell in place. Miriam wasn't the one that got away. It was Sierra. I had it all wrong. All those drunken nights on my back deck, I had it all wrong. It was the wrong girl. I have loved Sierra since I met her in high school and I just figured it out. It had slammed me in the mouth. No woman previous or prior will ever hold a candle to her. It has always been, Sierra Ostergard.

How I wanted to move down. But I was in the union at UPS and a full time job with full benefits was just around the corner. I couldn't let that go.

17

The following Sunday afternoon I was back home, and I was getting ready to go to the gym. I was fixing a pre-workout shake when Dad walked through the back door. He was whistling the MASH theme.

"Dad, I have found *THE ONE*."

"What?" He asked.

"Yup. The one."

"You mean, the one? The one and only?" He looked at me with wild anticipation. "You got a picture?" I showed him the selfie we took at Bailey's Pub on my birthday. "She have some Italian in her?"

"Yeah. She's half."

"I could tell. She's pretty."

"Yup. She's the one. I can't explain it."

"I know, it just hits you. I knew it the minute I met your mother." Dad said.

"I finally know what you were talking about when you talked about Mom like that." He seemed genuinely happy for me when I told him. He was happy anytime we mentioned my mother. He missed her every day. I now knew the pain he felt. I now knew how much he loved her because I feel it with Sierra. He lost that love and now I could imagine the hell he went through. "Yeah," he sighed, "it just hits you." He returned my phone to me. "I'm happy Shortstuff. You deserve it. I know you want a couple of monkeys running around."

"Yeah, that's a bit far off, but I know it. I found the one Dad."

Sierra and I talked on the phone every day. Any free moment we had about anything and everything. One night in the still twilight, I woke up and I couldn't breathe. The pain was horrendous. I couldn't sit still. The pain in my chest wasn't going away. I wanted to be with her every second. I missed waking up next to her. I missed her waking me up in the middle of the night to make love. I missed her smell. I missed her every little imperfection. I just missed her and I couldn't take it anymore.

There was a job opening at a U-Haul in Raleigh. So I applied for it. It was for Part-Time Assistant Manager. I interviewed with the General Manager long distance on the phone and unfortunately he filled it. The only thing he had was a part-time gig on Mechanical Boulevard in nearby Garner. I jumped on it.

"Dad, I'm moving!" I exclaimed on a warm and humid afternoon in July, 2010.

"Yeah? What'd you find, an apartment on the Boulevard?"

"No. I'm transferring to North Carolina through U-Haul to be a General Manager." I lied.

"What about UPS?" He asked.

"I'm moving on. No more UPS. I'm going to stay with Sierra when I get there."

Somehow, I think he knew I would be alright. He was calm, like he knew that I was where I was supposed to be in my life, and what I was to do next; move to North Carolina. "I hope you know what you're doing."

"I think I do."

"So you're gonna be head dog when you get down there. Your own store? Boss Hog?"

I shrugged. "Yeah, what idiots right?"

He laughed. He wasn't mad in the least. If I was with Pam or any other woman, he would have been upset at me for leaving a sure thing like UPS, or at least told me up front I was making a stupid move. But somehow I knew he thought I was going to be ok, all because of Sierra.

I told Sierra about the job transfer and we started planning my move. The truth was I had only scored an interview with the GM at the Garner location. I had no guarantee. But I had three years' experience at U-Haul. They would be stupid not to hire me.

18

On July 23, 2010, I strolled into UPS. Five years I worked there and for the first time the color was gone. I lost all motivation. I loved this job and that day, I realized it was all gone. I walked to the punch clock on the wall and Manny, my loading partner the last three years was leaning on the dock. We've knocked back some shine these past few years. He was a great dude.

I pecked my pin number in the keypad. "Well Manny, I believe today is my last day my brother."

He laughed. "Shut up Shorty, you're gonna retire here." He wore a cut off shirt sleeve as a headband to keep his mop of curly hair out of his eyes. He knew the debacle of my relationship with Pam. He also knew about my recent trip to North Carolina and Sierra.

"On Monday afternoon when I'm not here, talk to me then."

"I'll see you on Monday." He chuckled as we walked down the dock to the trailer we were scheduled to load.

"Yeah, I'm gonna miss this place."

He lit a cigarette and ducked into the bay door. "You love this place. You can check out, but you can never leave."

"Ok Don Henley, thanks."

"HA! You're the worst."

We loaded that trailer like any other night. We stacked packages, sang stupid songs, and sweat the night away. I miss working with that guy. He was real and he told you how it was. I miss all my friends from UPS. They were some of the best friends I ever had.

It's a dangerous place to be, the unknown. So I put all my chips on the table. I was all in.

EPILOGUE

1

I'm driving down Route 70 in downtown Mebane. The sun is long gone, and the wind blowing through my windows is a cool refreshing rinse. I turn the radio down as I pass Oscar's Oyster Bar on the corner where I turn toward Ashbury Apartments.

It is all familiar now. It's like I fit in where I'm accepted and loved. The twenty-seven year storm is over, and it has made me stronger.

I open the door to Sierra's studio apartment with the key she sent me just over two months ago. It is dark except for a flicker of candle light crawling from the bedroom area. She is in bed wearing a red nightie that looks ravishing on her. I stop at the foot of the bed. She looks at me with an anticipation I have seen many times in my dreams. In the candle light, I say to her what I have felt the last ten hours.

"I'm home baby."

2

I am tired. I spent the last twelve hours handling customer service and hitch installations and I'm ready to forget about it for a while. The sets of headlights on the interstate are NOT helping either. An hour drive home is something I NEVER look forward to after a day like this. But it's all I have right now to contribute. Something will come up; I'm a resourceful guy. But we're happy in our little studio apartment, and Sierra said that's all that matters. But I gotta keep making that paper.

The traffic on the I-40 westbound is pretty thick tonight, more than usual. The Durham Bulls played this afternoon and that is most likely the cause. It's a total of fourteen hours away from home, and it kills me. I never felt love like this. It's both excruciating and euphoric. My iPhone comes to life in my console.

"Hey Smirk."

"Hey." The phone says.

"Hey baby. What's going on?"

"Nothing, I just came from Mom's. How was your night?"

"Busy, installed three hitches tonight and Boss man left early so I had to run the joint for the last five hours."

"I'm sorry baby."

"It's all good. Don't apologize, it's not your fault."

"I got a present for you when you get home."

"You go shopping or something?"

"Yeah, I picked up a few things."

"Ok baby, I can't wait to get home. I'm tired let me tell ya, I just wanna lay on the chaise when I get home."

"Ok."

"Can I stop and get a sixer at the Lion King?"

"Come home first, we will go together. We need a few things from there anyway."

"Ok, sounds like a plan. I'll see ya when I get home."

"Ok, I love you."

"I love you too. More than you know." I break connection, throw my iPhone on the passenger seat, and keep driving. *Man, I can go for a Long Hammer IPA right about now. I can just about taste it.*

The sun was long gone by the time I turn into the apartment complex parking lot. *I sure remember the first time I turned into this parking lot a few short months prior to tonight. What a night that was.* I walk toward the front door and gaze to the sparse stars that are vibrant and bright tonight. The apartment complex is isolated on the block and the pool looks refreshing on this warm clear night in August.

I open the front door and Sierra is standing in the kitchenette slicing strawberries for a snack.

"Hey."

"Hey baby." I say, setting down my work bag by the front door. She leaves her strawberries to walk over and give me a hug. "Man, you are a sight for sore eyes."

"You saw me this morning and talked to me all day." She jokes.

"I know."

"I have a present for you."

"Yeah?" I ask.

She reaches around and grabs a small long box from the top of the kitchenette wall. The bow is white and flat. It looked like a necklace box.

"You bought me a necklace??"

She didn't answer. She stands there and looks up at me with a sly smile on her face. She likes to surprise me like this I have found out. I open the box to the expectation of finding a necklace. Why? I have no idea. I haven't worn a necklace since I was twenty-four. In the box is a home pregnancy test with a red "+" on it.

"Are you kidding me?!?" I ask. Sierra giggles but says nothing. "Are you KIDDING ME?" I pick her up and swing her around. Her hair smells like lavender.

It is the greatest surprise of my life.

"Are you excited?" I ask. The tears in my eyes make Sierra blurry. She is too quiet.

"Yes."

"So we're happy? We're gonna be parents? Me and you are gonna be parents? Someone is gonna call me Daddy someday?!?"

Sierra is giggling like a little girl. At this point I have forgotten about my day at U-Haul. My whole life is light years better with this news. I am going to be a father and the joy in my heart is almost too much to handle.

"I have had this news all morning. I took the first test this morning and when I saw the plus I immediately thought, 'Lucy'."

"You think we're having a girl?"

"Yeah."

"I don't know about all that. Let this sink in." Sierra exhales loudly and stands still. She looks up at me. "You ready?"

"Absolutely! I think I need a beer though. Can we go get beer?"

"Of course you can, Daddy."

She grabs the car keys off the dining room table and I turn and open the front door. Sierra turns off the lights and we walk out into the night air. We have a studio apartment that we rent for $500 a month. I work at a U-Haul with a two hour round trip commute for twenty hours at minimum wage with no benefits or health insurance. But I know that we're going to be ok. We have a child on the way and I find I am so excited I can't keep a single thought in my head. I have been taught to take care of what is close to you and now I'm going to have the family I always wanted.

Dad did his best. Sometimes it wasn't the right thing. But he taught what he knew. So did Cora. I can't blame her for the abuse. She did what she knew best for the situation she married into. I miss Grandpa every day and I'm sad our child will never meet him. If I said it once, I've said it a million times. If I turn out to be half the man my grandfather was, then I know I have succeeded.

Sierra and I got in her Jeep. I grab her hand and give it a light squeeze. "Hey Mommy." I say softly.

"Hey Daddy."

She put the Jeep in drive and we head off to get my beer.

AFTERWORD

In 1988, I was in fifth grade. There was this kid that wrote structured four page stories about a group of kids that hunted a shadowy killer. About halfway through the school year, he started simulating his friends as colorful characters in the story. It was brilliant! Soon after, my classmates and I were so enamored with being part of the story; we would pay him dimes and quarters to buy ourselves into the next episode. I ran out of money one week and I had accepted my fate after much debate. I told him to give me a noble death. I ended up getting blown to smithereens saving three characters.

Through that experience, I started writing short stories of my own. I was banned from watching "Nightmare on Elm Street" movies which was all the rage at the time. Everyone in school talked about seeing them, (probably by word of mouth because they were banned from watching themselves and didn't want to look uncool), so I wrote a story called "Tales of Freddy." I thought it was awesome despite the blatant plagiarism. Years later, I would write about zombies, aliens, and strange things. I grew up with Stephen King novels, it was bound to happen.

In high school, I wrote certain ideas down and set them aside for a later date. Now I'm glad I did because I'm ready to bring these characters to life.

When my wife and I started dating, one night we talked about literary characters and books we loved. We talked about classic literature and how much of it we had missed out on. We made a pact to rectify that. I read

"Catcher in the Rye" by J.D. Salinger and I fell in love with it. Holden Caulfield, the prick that he was, reminded me of myself when I was in high school. He was the quintessential boy at that age. This was where Shorty Benton came to life.

"Straight Ahead, In the Dark," is my "Catcher in the Rye."

S. M. Bailey
September 1, 2015

ACKNOWLEDGEMENTS

I would like to thank Brima Lamin, for without your persistence, I would have given up on this like I do everything else.

Leslie Greathouse, for your kind words, editing, and input.

Pam Dixon, Charisse Shanahan and Shannon Bailey for introducing me to Stephen King and being the motherly figures I needed growing up.

Rich Bailey, for inspiring me to write this story.

Sarah Bailey, my wife, for proofreading and making sure my writing isn't horrendous.

Made in the USA
Lexington, KY
07 November 2015